WRONG

An avid reader with a passion for creative writing and storytelling, **Shilpa Suraj** participated in writing competitions at school and dabbled in copy writing for an ad agency as a teenager. Twenty years in the corporate space, including a stint in corporate communications for Google India, and a spell at entrepreneurship, all hold her in good stead. A mother, she is currently the head of human resources and public relations at an architecture and interior design firm. She is also the author of *Saved by Love*, *Driven by Desire* and *Insta Reddy*.

WRONG

Shilpa Suraj

RUPA

Published by
Rupa Publications India Pvt. Ltd 2022
7/16, Ansari Road, Daryaganj
New Delhi 110002

Sales centres:
Allahabad Bengaluru Chennai
Hyderabad Jaipur Kathmandu
Kolkata Mumbai

Copyright © Shilpa Suraj 2022

This is a work of fiction. Names, characters, places and
incidents are either the product of the author's imagination or are
used fictitiously and any resemblance to any actual person, living or dead,
events or locales is entirely coincidental.

All rights reserved.
No part of this publication may be reproduced, transmitted,
or stored in a retrieval system, in any form or by any means,
electronic, mechanical, photocopying, recording or otherwise,
without the prior permission of the publisher.

P-ISBN: 978-93-5520-896-5
E-ISBN: 978-93-5520-898-9

First impression 2022

10 9 8 7 6 5 4 3 2 1

The moral right of the author has been asserted.

Printed in India

This book is sold subject to the condition that it shall not,
by way of trade or otherwise, be lent, resold, hired out, or otherwise
circulated, without the publisher's prior consent, in any form of
binding or cover other than that in which it is published.

To Zoe,

*In all the 'wrong' that life threw at me,
you were the 'right' that blazed a shining
trail through it…*

Prologue

'We need to talk.'

Ananya kept her eyes trained on the patch of road illuminated by the headlights of the car.

'Hmm?'

Arvin's absent-minded response left her clenching her mehendi-stained hands in her lap.

'I can't marry you,' she blurted out before her already faltering courage failed her completely. 'I can't marry you.' The words came out easier the second time. She exhaled shakily, a weight lifting off her shoulders.

'What?' He laughed, surprise coating his voice. 'Is this some kind of a silly pre-wedding prank?'

'No.' She continued to stare at the empty stretch of road in front of them.

'This isn't funny, Ananya.'

'Do I look like I'm joking?' Finally, she took her eyes off the road and looked at him. The hard, disbelieving look he threw her left everything inside her quaking. She was about to press the timer on the bomb that was going to explode everything she'd known in her life so far. She trembled as she took another deep breath.

'I'm in love with someone else.'

The silence that filled the car didn't hold a candle to the fear inside her as she finally managed to say what was bubbling up inside her. She was in love with someone else.

Arvin sat beside her as if turned to stone. He was the man her parents and the rest of the world deemed perfect for her. He was the fiancé who, until the last second, had been one of her closest friends.

Oh God, what had she done?

A lorry drove past them, horn blaring. It was the only noise that broke the silence in the car.

'Say something,' she whispered finally. 'Please say something.'

Still nothing. A man urinating by the roadside made an obscene gesture at them as they zoomed past. Ananya kept her gaze focussed out of the window until his voice broke the quiet.

'Who is it?'

She couldn't tell him just yet. The betrayal was too huge. Swallowing the lump in her throat, she lied, 'No one you know.'

'We've known each other a long time now. How is it possible that I don't know this guy?'

'He's someone I've met recently.' This at least was the truth, to an extent.

Arvin laughed, disbelievingly. 'You're throwing away everything we have over someone you've just met?'

How could she explain? She found it hard to understand herself.

'He,' she stammered, her heart quailing at the look in his eyes. 'He makes me feel...' Knowing there was no way to sugarcoat it, she blurted it out, 'He makes me feel so much more than I ever expected to.' Putting her palm across her chest as if to stop her thudding heart, she added, 'I've never felt this way about anyone before and—'

'Spare me the melodrama,' Arvin snapped. *'We're good together, Ananya. That's why our families set us up. We're friends who complement each other on every level. You're going to throw it all away because some random guy got your hormones all fired up?'*

'It isn't like that.' Temper swirled with guilt within her. 'I love him. I'm sorry it happened this way, but—'

'Nothing has happened.' Wrenching the steering wheel violently to avoid a huge ditch, he added, 'Nothing. Do you understand me? We're getting married in two days and that's final. I will not be made a laughingstock in front of the entire world.'

'You can't force me,' she retorted, her stubbornness rising to the fore.

'Goddammit, Ananya, you're ruining both our lives over—' His words drowned out the high-pitched squeal of brakes being jammed. The tyres screeched. Metal met metal in a sickening clang. There was screaming. She didn't realize it was her until the pain hit. Violent, raw, furious pain. And then nothing.

Ananya came awake with a gasp. Drenched with sweat, she fumbled for the bottle of water kept on her nightstand and then took a large gulp the second she managed to open the cap. She continued breathing heavily, making desperate attempts to slow her heartbeat.

Her gaze fell on Arvin sleeping next to her. Her handsome, successful husband. Safe and peaceful. Unintentionally, her gaze travelled down to the foot of the bed. Arvin's worn, comfortable shorts stretched over his muscular thighs, one of which ended with only one leg.

She then glanced at his prosthetic, which was propped up by the bed within easy reach if he needed anything for the night. Her eyes took in the ugly scar tissue just above the otherwise smooth stump.

She'd done this to him. She was the reason he lived in pain every day, every hour, every minute. It was only fair that she, too, felt the pain. And so, she had married him.

She was alive and unharmed. It did not matter that she loved another man. She loved with a fierceness that brought nothing but pain, a pain that she deserved. She'd chosen this life. Arvin was both her husband and her penance.

Chapter 1

'Dear Arnav,

How are you? I have to ask you something. Please don't say no. Will you come home? I know you don't want to, but will you come anyway? I need you. I need my family. Please come.

Love,

Ma'

༄

'Arnav's back.'

Freezing, with her fingers on the zipper of her dress, Ananya met her husband's eyes in the mirror. Swallowing to wet her suddenly dry throat, she managed a nonchalant, 'Oh?'

'He'll be staying with us. Have a room readied.' Completely unaware of the fact that he'd sent his wife's world into a tailspin, Arvin reached for his bottle of cologne.

Keeping her face carefully expressionless, Ananya asked, 'For how long?'

'Sorry?' With his mind already on the next morning's meeting, Arvin shot his cuffs and checked his reflection in the mirror his wife sat in front of. Tonight's party was important. The CEO of a company he'd set his sights on for a very long time was attending, and no one wined and dined the opposition better than Arvin Saxena.

'How long will Arnav be here for?' His wife's husky voice broke through his mental strategizing.

'I don't know.' Irritated at her interruption, he snapped, 'He's my brother. I'm not going to ask him when he's leaving the day he arrives.'

'I'm only asking so that I can make arrangements for his stay.' Keeping her face averted from his, Ananya fastened the clasp on her watch and took her time selecting her perfume for the evening. Her hand hovered for a microsecond over her favourite Chanel before moving on to the Dior bottle next to it. Spraying some of it, she let the fragrance settle her frazzled nerves.

Face a serene mask, she slipped her feet into crystal-studded stilettoes and rose from her seat. Even with the added advantage of the heels, she barely came up to her tall husband's broad shoulders. Dispassionately, she took in the sight of them framed in the mirror. His perfectly tailored grey suit fit his gym-toned body to perfection and proved the perfect foil for her simple, black dress that skimmed her slender figure. They were one of the country's power couples—a match that had married two of the most influential families in India. They were perfect.

But now there was one wrinkle in their otherwise smooth life: Arnav.

'What are you wearing?' The sound of Arvin's irritated voice snapped her out of her thoughts.

Raising an eyebrow, she glanced at her inoffensive black

dress. There was nothing wrong with it. It was simple, chic and elegant. A liquid column of silk that ended at her ankles and let her crystal-studded stilettos peep out from the bottom.

'A dress?' The taunt slipped out before she could rein in her wayward tongue.

'You look like a nun.' He stormed over to her wardrobe and yanked the door open. He could see rows of dresses arranged by their colours. Some even had their tags on. Rifling through them till he found what he wanted, he pulled out a grey dress and threw it across the bed.

'Change.'

The snapped order had her spine stiffening. She could almost feel it locking into place, one vertebra at a time.

'Why?'

The question infuriated him. 'When I ask you to do something, you don't question it. Do you understand? You do what I tell you, when I tell you.'

Or what? The words danced at the tip of her tongue, but Ananya swallowed them. She knew better than to start a fight before they had to make a public appearance.

Picking up the grey dress, she disappeared into the bathroom adjoining their room. Decorated with a combination of Italian marble and handcrafted tiles, and hosting enough mirrors to please any exhibitionist, the bathroom could have easily housed a family of three. Turning her back on the Jacuzzi fitted in the corner, she faced one of the floor-length mirrors and quickly changed into the grey dress.

Looking at her reflection in the mirror, she knew why her husband had chosen it. Modestly covering her chest, it left her nearly naked from the back. Tears stung the back of her eyes, but she furiously blinked them back before they could spill and ruin her carefully applied makeup. When other people would see them tonight, they would see a happily married couple and a broad-minded husband who stood proudly by his wife. Ananya knew better. Arvin wasn't showing off his wife, he was flaunting his whore.

∽

There was a special place in hell for men who were in love with another man's wife. Arnav contemplated the fifteen-year-old Scotch in the crystal glass in front of him. It helped fan the flames of the hellfire in his gut. It didn't stop his gaze from being drawn to the back of her dress. The outfit shimmered like silver smoke over her lithe body. He could see her husband's hand resting possessively on her exposed back, a thumb gently gliding over her creamy, unblemished skin.

He clenched his glass and gulped down almost half of its contents, savouring the burning trail it left inside him. It did nothing for the guilt that was his constant companion, but it numbed the pain that clawed through him, be it only for a moment.

She laughed. It was a tinkling burst of sound that cut through the quiet murmur of the sophisticated, high society crowd that had gathered for the charity event. A few tendrils of her hair escaped the complicated hairdo her glorious waist-length mane was caught up in and flirted with the nape of her neck.

Cursing, he pushed back from the table. He needed a smoke and he didn't care if the world thought it was rude of him to walk out right now.

As he made his way through the throng, a part of

him registered the way she leaned against her husband and murmured something into his ear. Turning towards her, he gave her an indulgent smile that spoke volumes about their relationship.

Oh yes, there was a special place in hell for men who loved another man's wife. He breathed, crawled and existed in that abyss, for he didn't just love another man's wife, he loved his brother's wife. Amidst the scum that grew in the filthy gutter of the deepest, darkest bowels of hell, he was the slime you scraped off the bottom of your shoe. He lived and breathed guilt, remorse and gut-searing pain. She was his friend, his passion, his endless torment, his curse. And yet, he loved her.

∽

'Arnav.'

His mother's voice had him turning to face her. Shayla Saxena stood framed in the doorway. The simple cream-coloured saree she wore did nothing to disguise the fact that it probably cost the equivalent of most people's monthly wages.

'Why are you out here in the balcony?' She came to stand next to him. Her fingers gently clasped the railing as she looked up at the night sky. There wasn't much to see. Shrouded in pollution and thick clouds, there wasn't a star in sight. Arnav's steady stream of smoke rings didn't help either. The patterns of those smoke rings were familiar to her.

He hadn't answered her question. She pretended not to notice. That, too, was a pattern she was familiar with. Shayla sighed. She loved her family. She truly did, but some days they were so much work.

'It's been a very warm winter so far.' She tried to strike up a conversation with him. Four long years. It had been four very long years since she'd seen her son. He had left the day after Arvin's wedding. His body language told her it wouldn't take much to have him pack his bags and leave again.

'Hmm.'

It was an answer of sorts. She wished she knew how to reach out to him. He'd left home when he was barely eighteen, had refused to join his father's business and had instead started his own. Her heart still ached thinking of the conflict that decision had given rise to in the family, the hurtful words and the allegations that father and son had flung at each other. Though he stayed in touch with her through letters and calls all those years, he rarely came home.

She'd visited him as often as she could, but her husband's barely concealed disapproval had made sure that she didn't as often as she wished to. He had left that night following the fallout with his father and had returned only for his younger brother's wedding. She had been thrilled to have her family back under one roof. Even her husband had been willing to try, to let bygones be bygones. After all, Arvin had joined the business and was making such an incredible mark. He had a son who was fulfilling his dreams, so he could be forgiving and magnanimous with the one who hadn't. But things had gone wrong again. She just didn't know how or what had happened.

Arnav had always been a loner, but now he had turned into a recluse. If there was a magic wand, Shayla would have waved it to find out what had driven her son away, away from all of them.

It had taken tears, cajoling and in the end the make-believe excuse of a weak heart for her to convince him to come home for a visit again. Lost in thought, she was still mulling the best way to approach her son about what she had in mind when he finally spoke.

'You don't actually have a heart problem, do you?'

Shayla was startled. Guilt had her averting her eyes from his. 'Umm actually, sometimes it starts beating so fast…'

Arnav couldn't stop himself from laughing. His mother looked like a guilty schoolgirl who'd been caught sneaking a smoke.

'That's probably anxiety attacks as a result of living with Dad.'

'Arnav!' The gentle remonstration in her tone had him shrugging unapologetically. There was no love lost between his father and him, and that was a fact everyone knew. His mother may not want to acknowledge it, but she couldn't ignore it either. He had made his peace with the fact. He loved the family he was born into, all acrimony aside, but he had found his true family in the life he'd built away from them, in his friends and in his work. He had followed his passion and didn't have a moment's regret over his decisions. There wasn't a thing inside that room that he missed or craved.

But a person maybe… He could not and he would not think about that now, about her.

'I'm glad you came home, Arnav.' His mother's wistful voice broke through his pained contemplation. Guilt had him putting his arm around her shoulder and drawing her close.

'Stay for a while this time, please.'

'I have taken a month off.' He hesitated to say he could stay longer if he wanted to. 'I'll be here for a while.'

Shayla interpreted the information as 'only a month'.

If that was all she was to get of her son's time, she would make the most of it.

'Did you meet Arvin?' she asked.

'Briefly.' His baby brother had been too busy for anything more than a cursory greeting.

'And Ananya?'

Bitter hurt lanced through him at the sound of her name. Bracing himself, he answered, 'Yes.'

'She's lovely, isn't she?' There was genuine affection in her voice.

'Lovely,' he agreed, though the words tasted like mud in his mouth.

'I should get back inside. Your father must be waiting for me. Come in, Arnav.' Letting her fingers rest lightly on his arm, she said, 'Come in and join the party. Join us.'

Taking her hand from his arm, he kissed her palm lightly. 'In a while,' he promised. 'I need a little time to myself.'

With a light kiss on his cheek, she rejoined the party. She'd done her best. Now it was up to him if he wanted to be a part of the world around him or hold himself away from it all, like he always did. Looking back, she saw him continue to lean against the railing and stare out into the night. She knew it was probably time to accept defeat. He had made his choice a long time ago. There was no bringing him back, no matter how hard she tried.

But then again, she had the coming month. She wouldn't give up yet.

Chapter 2

Laughter rang through the hall as Arnav let himself in through the door. He paused and looked around. People didn't laugh like that in Saxena House. Bemused, he walked down the corridor and looked into the drawing room.

She was the latest addition to the family, he supposed. She had her back to him, so all he was left with was a glimpse of her long hair falling almost till her waist, and a pretty pink salwar kameez, which he was sure cost as much as his entire month's grocery bill.

'Arnav.' His mother's excited voice cut through his thoughts. 'Finally, you're here.'

Arnav sighed. He had just arrived and was starting to hate every minute of it already. Pasting a polite smile on his face, he stepped into the room and greeted his mother. Leaning down, he kissed her cheek before turning to hug his brother, who strode over to thump him on his back. With his father, who sat in the corner and watched them, he exchanged a cold nod.

'Ananya,' his brother, Arvin, called out, 'come meet my brother.'

'Finally,' she said, with the same lilting laugh that had caught his attention.

She casually looped a hand through Arvin's arm and surveyed him. 'I thought Arvin had made you up.'

Arnav smiled, stiffly, as his brother's new fiancée sized him up in front of everyone. There was nothing insulting about it. He wondered whether his family had told her anything about him. If they hadn't, it was probably for the best. He doubted whether they even had anything to tell her. It surely couldn't have been anything good, he thought.

Someone in the crowded room called out to Arvin and he left to speak with them. His mother gave a slight smile and wandered off towards some of her relatives. He was now left to make small talk with his soon-to-be sister-in-law.

Arnav sighed.

'I'm not that bad.' The amused comment had him glancing at her. She grinned. Her open, infectious smile had him smiling back. She wasn't classically beautiful, but there was something extremely engaging about her. Her beauty was something that would grow on you over the years. But her smile...the smile and the cheerful warmth she exuded tipped her over from pretty to gorgeous. Arvin was a lucky man.

'I know,' he answered. 'It's just that I am.'

She laughed. 'You can't be all that bad.'

'I'm a beast,' he confessed, 'and on that note, I'm going to have to excuse myself. I want to go shower and make myself presentable for dinner.'

'Sure. I—' Whatever she was going to say trailed off when she looked over his shoulder. Her smile widened even further, if that was possible. 'Papa, can I get you something? Another drink?'

Arnav's smile disappeared. He turned, cautiously, and found himself face to face with his father.

'Yes.' His father nodded, holding his glass out to her.

'I'll get it.' Arnav took the glass, irritated by his father's attitude towards his new daughter-in-law. But then, Akhilesh Saxena thought the whole world existed to serve him.

'No. Don't bother!' Ananya exclaimed. 'I'll get it. I was the one who offered.'

'Let him,' Akhilesh spoke. 'Let him go pour my drink and bring it. He likes doing this kind of work anyway. Till now, he wanted to be a cook. Maybe he has decided to be a bartender next.'

As Arnav was facing her, he saw her expression change at his father's callous comment. He caught the flash of anger that lit her eyes before disappearing. Her mouth tightened at the corners, but she held her smile.

'Coffee, Tea or Me, right?' she asked.

Startled, Arnav nodded.

'I ate there with my friends a year ago. I was holidaying in Mumbai and they dragged me to the hottest new café in town.' She closed her eyes. There was a reminiscent smile on her lips. 'Your chicken kiev was a masterpiece and that coffee soufflé, oh my God! I'm drooling just thinking about it.'

Opening her eyes, she looked over his shoulder and beamed at his father. 'He's an artist, Papa, with magic in his fingers. I know you must be very proud. How could you not be?'

Reaching across Arnav, she took the glass from a silent Akhilesh. 'I'll get you your drink. I don't know about Arnav, but I've always fancied being a bartender.'

She was gone a second later. Akhilesh seemed dumbfounded. Arnav...Arnav was left reeling under the realization that someone had actually defended him. It was a strange feeling for someone who'd always stood alone, fighting his own battles.

Arnav stopped his slightly battered older sedan next to the parade of luxury vehicles parked in the massive garage. Stepping out, he grabbed the duffle bag he'd stashed in the rear seat. It quite literally contained all the clothes he owned. He was not a hoarder.

He stopped and looked up at the mansion in front of him. The clever use of brick and ivy on the outside gave it a warm cottage atmosphere that belied the sheer size of it. This should have been home, but it had not been for far too many years. His mind dragged him back to the last time he'd come home for a visit. Too much had happened during that trip and even more since then.

Shutting the door on the memories swarming through his brain, he shouldered his bag and strode forward. He was here for one reason—his mother. He was going to grit his teeth and get through the next month, so he could disappear from their lives for another few years with a clear conscience.

He was halfway up the drive when he heard a car roaring up behind him. The red two-seater convertible came to a stop a few feet away from him. As if by magic, a househelp materialized from the side of the house and rushed to open the car door. Slim legs encased in sober black trousers and ending in comfortable dark silver ballet flats emerged from behind the car door. A second later, she was standing in front of him. Her tucked-in tailored white shirt fit her to perfection. Her hair was twined back in a complicated braid and she had her sunglasses perched on top of her head. With her attention on the phone in her hand, she reached back into the car and grabbed a laptop bag. Tipping her sunglasses forward, she covered her eyes, while continuing to read something on her phone screen.

A sardonic smile touched his lips as he continued to be ignored by both the staff and the mistress. The devil riding his shoulder had him planting his feet and staying where he was. She was still frowning at her phone when she walked full tilt into him.

'Oh.' The startled sound escaped her as she collided with him.

'Hello, Anni.'

Her entire body stiffened at the nickname. Had he been the fanciful sort, he would have sworn she'd pulled on some invisible armour. Luckily, he'd lost every hint of fancy when he'd lost her, when they'd destroyed everything they were to each other.

'Ananya,' she corrected him.

Yes, she was Ananya now. There was no trace of his Anni left in her. Gone was the wide, warm smile, the laughing eyes, the tight bear hugs. Calm, cool and controlled as she was, she made him itch to ruffle that composure.

'*Sharmaji, Sahib ke samaan upar wale kamre mein rakh dijiye* (Sharmaji, please shift Sahib's luggage to the room upstairs).'

And with that one command, she put him in his place. She was the regal hostess to this unwanted guest. Acknowledging the subtle reminder with a faint smile, he stepped aside for her to precede him up the driveway. His gaze roved over her as she walked ahead of him.

'Kitty party?' he queried, more out of a desire to irritate her than to make conversation.

She didn't bother replying. The front doors, which they'd reached, magically opened. Must be another one of the minions scurrying to welcome the princess of their little fiefdom, he supposed. They'd just stepped in when he heard his mother's delighted voice.

'Arnav, you're back!' She hurried down the stairs towards where the two of them still stood. 'What was the need to go stay with a friend after the party yesterday?' she scolded him.

He figured telling her he felt more welcomed at his friend's place was not a very wise idea. So, he said nothing, but leaned forward and dutifully kissed his mother's cheek instead.

'Ananya, you're home early.' She turned to her daughter-in-law with a beaming smile. 'I'm so glad. Now the entire family is here together.'

The *entire* family? *Christ.* Now he would have to deal with his father before he'd managed to get even a fortifying cup of coffee.

'The judge took ill suddenly, so our hearing was postponed. I had some free time and thought I'd come home for lunch.' Her husky voice brought his attention back to the conversation.

So, she was finally putting her law degree to use. That was a surprise. He wouldn't have thought that his father would have allowed his daughter-in-law to work, and especially the one who was married to his favourite son.

'I need to get back to the office post lunch though,' she added.

'Yes. Of course. Of course.' His mother fussed around them in an uncharacteristic show of nerves. But then his father tended to bring out the worst in all of them, Arnav mused.

He followed the women past the cavernous drawing room and into the formal dining room ahead to be greeted by a scene that was both familiar and new at the same time. Akhilesh sat at the head of the dining table that could seat sixteen. To his right, Arvin sat with an iPad. Going by the frown on his face, whatever he was reading was not good news.

The rest of the table was empty but had been set meticulously, right down to the crystal glassware and what looked like plates from a heritage collection. An array of dishes filled with food lined the table, most of which looked like they hadn't been touched.

'Look who's here,' his mother trilled.

Arnav winced at the hint of desperation in her voice. He wished she wouldn't try so hard. That his father despised him was no secret and he'd grown a thick enough hide to convince himself he no longer cared. The man in question looked up for a brief moment, nodded and went back to his newspaper.

'Hi, Bhai.'

Arnav smiled, acknowledging his brother's greeting. They would catch up later when their father wasn't glowering at them. He waited for the ladies to take their places before sitting down.

Ananya walked over to sit next to Arvin. Turning her plate over, she thanked the househelp who was filling her glass with water. His mother sat down to his father's left, leaving Arnav with no choice but to take the seat next to her, the one opposite Ananya.

'Rice or roti?'

His mother's question was buried underneath his father's brusque one.

'How long are you here for?'

'I have about a month free.'

A loud thud was heard as Ananya's glass fell on the dining table, spilling water all over Arvin's iPad. He started to curse, shaking his iPad to try and drain the excess water.

'You clumsy idiot.'

The snarled insult had Arnav rising from his chair before he recalled where he was. Still, he stayed on his feet, watching carefully as Ananya apologized profusely. Arvin brushed away her calming hand in an irritable gesture.

His mother's hand tugged at Arnav's and had him slowly sitting again.

'Enough.' His father's voice cracked across the noise and had everyone subsiding into silence.

'Are you prepared for the Biosphere meeting?' he addressed his younger son, who was still trying to rein in his temper.

'Yes.' He nodded curtly. 'They'll agree to our terms.'

'Good.'

And with that the conversation stayed on the most important part of the family. The Ariaa Group of Hotels. Arnav's grandfather had started the first one in Delhi and his father had expanded that to three more in Mumbai, Cochin and Bangalore. From his mother's last email, it looked like his brother was planning to grow the business overseas, Singapore, to be precise.

Keeping his gaze carefully averted from Ananya's pale face, he let his mother fuss over him and overload his plate with more food than any normal person could possibly eat.

∽

A month! He was here to stay for a month. Frustration and anguish swirled within her as she recalled Arnav's gravelly voice when he said those damned words. Ananya stared at the file in front of her. She'd been looking at the blasted thing for over half an hour now and hadn't processed a single word.

She took a deep breath and tried to refocus. Her clients deserved her complete attention. She read through the file for the umpteenth time. A woman had come forward alleging rape by her father-in-law. Not surprisingly, neither her mother-in-law nor her husband were willing to support her claim.

Thankfully, her parents had stepped up and were backing her in court. As she read through the evidence and statements filed, Ananya kept an open mind. It wasn't unusual for women nowadays to take advantage of the laws drafted to keep them physically and financially safe. Her firm specialized in dowry harassment and domestic violence cases but always went an extra mile to ensure the cases were genuine.

As she read, she made notes. Engrossed in the sordid saga unfolding in the file in front of her, it took her a minute to realize someone was knocking on her office door. Frowning, she strode over to yank it open. Her staff knew better than to interrupt her when her door was shut.

'What is—'

The rest of her words died on her lips at the sight of Arvin standing there. Dread pooled in the pit of her stomach as it always did when her husband paid her an unexpected visit. It generally didn't bode well for her.

Stepping back in silent invitation, she waited till he entered the room before shutting the door behind him. The less her colleagues heard of this conversation, the better.

He walked in with the innate confidence she'd once found so appealing. A familiar disparaging look around her simple office had her stiffening. He chose to stand rather than sit in the plastic chair, meant for visitors, in front of her desk.

Ignoring the condescending vibes emanating from him, Ananya sat down behind her desk and smiled. 'This is a nice surprise.'

'You need to take some time off work.'

Her smile died. She had a full caseload on her hands, and she would be damned if she disappointed the women who depended on her, all just to entertain his stupid whims.

'No.'

'No?' He smiled. 'I wasn't asking you. I was telling you.'

'I can't take time off right now.' She didn't bother asking for the reason behind his command. She wasn't going to leave from her office when several of her cases were at such crucial junctures. 'My cases—'

'I don't care.'

When did you ever? She banished the bitter thought immediately. She knew that if she opened that door, she would not be able to get through even one day of her life.

'Arvin, please.' She hated the plea in her tone, but knew there was a slim chance he would listen to her if she humiliated herself enough.

'Please?' A mocking smile told her it wasn't going to work today. 'Take the next week off. We're flying to Singapore. I have some important business meetings there and it's important my loving wife is by my side for all the social events.'

A wave of helpless rage surged through her. Temper had her getting to her feet to face him. 'You came all the way down to my office to tell me this? It couldn't have waited till I got home?'

'I wanted to make sure you did as I said.' Stepping back, he pulled open the door. 'Let's go have a chat with your boss.'

'No.' She didn't move. 'I'll speak to her.'

'Come on, sweetheart.' The endearment made her want to throw something at his head. 'I'm here to support you and smooth things over with your boss.'

'You're here to make me look flighty and frivolous,' she managed to say through gritted teeth. 'She's going to think I'm not capable of doing anything unless my rich husband is there to hold my hand.'

This job was all she had—the one part of her life that brought her happiness, the one place no one saw her as a rich, pampered bimbo.

'It's all about perception, isn't it?' he grinned.

'Why, Arvin?' Exhaustion seeped into her voice. 'You're going to get me fired. Why are you doing this to me?'

'You really need to ask?' His voice hardened.

'We were friends once. The best of friends. Have you forgotten?'

'I haven't forgotten a damn thing. Have you?' The furious hurt in his voice had her flinching.

'Haven't I paid enough?' She had already given him the rest of her life. What else was left to give?

'You ruined my life,' he spat at her. 'Nothing will ever be enough.'

'I married you. I'll stay married to you. I'll do whatever you ask of me as your wife. Please, just let me have my job. Let me keep this one part of my life.' She would have dropped to her knees had that helped. 'Please, Arvin, I'm begging you.'

He stared at her for a long moment. Hope flared in a small part of her heart. Just when she was about to speak again, he said, 'I have an important meeting to get back to. Let's not keep your boss waiting any longer.'

Hours later, she lay in bed, staring at the ceiling. Arvin snored next to her. He was so loud that she felt like someone was drilling a hole in her head. She got up, sidestepped his artificial leg and left the bedroom for the drawing room that adjoined it.

Curling up on the couch, she tried to fall asleep. However, she wound up feeling more awake than before. She gave up and went in search of something to drink. A hot mug of milk would help her relax.

The meeting with her boss, to which Arvin accompanied her, had been just as disastrous as she'd expected. Her boss's tirade still rang in her ears. Ananya had struggled to find a firm that would accept her for who she was and not for whom she was married to. It had taken time, but she'd finally got a job in the field of her choice. But now it looked like she wouldn't have it for long.

She'd got the week off accompanied by a stiff, disapproving lecture on learning to take her work seriously. She was told that if all she wanted to do was go gallivanting around the world, then she should sit at home and let another deserving lawyer take her place.

She had taken the dressing-down quietly, knowing it was well deserved. She had four days remaining to work overtime and make sure the colleague filling in for her had only the bare minimum to do the next week. She was determined to show her boss that she wasn't flighty and irresponsible, even if Arvin went out of his way to portray her in that light.

Turning on the light in the kitchen, she pulled out the carton of milk and poured some into a mug. She left it to warm in the microwave and rooted around for the biscuit tin. When she found the chocolate chip cookies, she almost wept with gratitude.

Whatever else might disappear from her life, she knew she would always have chocolate. Biting into one, she retrieved her mug and turned only to walk into a broad chest. A familiar one. The hot milk splattered all over his bare skin.

'I'm so sorry.' Face flaming, she grabbed a napkin and futilely tried to wipe off the milk. 'Did you get burnt?'

'No.' Arnav caught her hand that was still fluttering over his chest. 'I'm fine.' He reached behind her and grabbed a cookie for himself.

'Why are you wandering around the house so late?'

'Why are you walking around half naked?'

They spoke at the same time, words tumbling over each others'. Ananya tried hard to regain her composure but couldn't with all that warm, taut skin on display.

Doesn't the stupid man own clothes? Who walks around a house in just boxers, especially when he knows he isn't alone in the damn house? His parents, too, live here, for God's sake.

His parents would have probably already seen a lot more of him, and for that matter, so had she. Her face flamed at the errant thought.

'I'm sorry.' His quiet voice cut through her rambling thoughts. 'I didn't think anybody else would be awake at this time.'

She didn't reply. She should have taken what was remaining of her milk and left. But she did not move. She found that she couldn't.

'You've been crying.'

He was the first person to notice, the only person to ever

notice. She couldn't afford to let him break down the walls she had so carefully built around her.

'Are you okay, Anni?'

The soft murmur stroked her battered heart. How long had it been since someone had asked her that question? How long had it been since someone had cared for her?

'Anni?' That damn bare chest was back in her line of vision. All she wanted to do was wrap herself around it and sob.

'Ananya.' Her voice shook for a second, but she regained control of it quickly. 'My name is Ananya. It would be best if you remembered that.'

And then she moved past him, past his quiet concern, past his steady warmth. She kept moving away from it all and into the cold, into the cruel.

Chapter 3

'Oh shit!'

Arnav froze. The cigarette he had just placed between his lips fell to the floor. Retrieving it, he glanced at the shadowy corner and saw the future daughter-in-law of the Saxena family stub out her own cigarette with her heel.

'If you tell your brother, the wedding is off,' she said, coming forward to join him near the railing that bordered the terrace.

'He doesn't know you smoke?'

'He does.' She exhaled, wrapping her arms around her midriff. 'He thinks I'm quitting.'

'Are you?' Arnav leaned back against the railing and lit another cigarette for himself.

'I want to.' Ananya stared at the city lights sprawled in front of them. 'I seem to lack the will power to do it.' She then laughed and said, 'You must think I'm awful.'

'Why?' Arnav took a deep drag and exhaled. He could feel some of the tightness inside him, which always accompanied his interactions with his family, ease with each breath.

'I'm lying to your brother, my fiancé,' she pointed out.

Arnav shrugged. 'That's between the two of you.'

'If people find out I smoke, I'd be sullying the family name,' she said with a hint of a question in her voice.

'Sully away.' Arnav waved a hand in the air. 'From what my father continually points out, there isn't anything left to sully after the damage I've done to it.'

She laughed, a delighted burst of sound that had him smiling, too. They stood for a while in companionable silence, staring out into the night.

'Stop that,' Arnav said.

'What?' she asked after a moment. 'I haven't done anything.'

'Stop trying to inhale my cigarette smoke from the side. I can hear those deep breaths of yours. You sound like an out-of-control beagle.'

'An out-of-control beagle? That's the best you could come up with?' Ananya giggled.

Offering her a cigarette from the pack stashed in his pocket, Arnav grinned, 'It's late, I'm tired and I didn't think you'd appreciate being called a phone sex operator.'

'I would make an excellent phone sex operator,' she replied nonchalantly. Leaning closer to him, she cupped a palm around the tip of his cigarette and lit hers.

Arnav froze. Something stirred within him as he looked down at her smiling face. Desire slammed through him an instant later as she tilted her head back and closed her eyes. The sweet, blissful look on her face warmed the cold spaces inside him, spaces he had forgotten about until now. But this was his brother's fiancée. The thought was enough to douse his ardour.

Shifting slightly away from her, he contemplated the glowing tip of his cigarette. He had already been a lousy son and an absentee brother, but lusting after his soon-to-be sister-in-law was wrong on a whole other level.

'Why did you want to become a chef?'

The idle question pulled him from his thoughts. Wondering

why she wanted to know, he answered, 'Cooking relaxes me and growing up, I needed to relax. Our house was…'

He stopped mid-sentence, unsure if he should be sharing this with her.

'I know what it was like,' she said softly. 'Arvin's told me.'

Of course, he had. His brother would have wanted to warn his bride about the family she was marrying into. Shaking off the mood that gripped him, Arnav said lightly, 'I also figured that it would piss my father off more than any other career choice.'

She laughed. 'And was it worth it?'

Arnav thought about it barely for a second. 'Yes.'

'Why did you choose law?' It was his turn to ask. The urge to know more about her was hard to resist.

'I don't like being in the grey,' she said after a pause. 'The black-and-white nature of the job appealed to me.'

'You're joking, right?' He turned to stare at her. 'Lawyers swim in the grey. They wouldn't know black and white if it hit them in the face.'

'True,' she acknowledged. 'But that's a personal choice, isn't it? And I've chosen to honour the law, to fight fairly, to champion the underdogs. It might sound like a cliché. I've been born into privilege. I know it. I accept it. But that doesn't mean I have to just sit back and enjoy it. I want to use it to make a difference.'

Arnav looked away from her. He needed to leave, get back to his room, shut the door and forget the fact that he was attracted to his brother's fiancée. He repeated the last few words in his head over and over again.

'Also, I really like to argue.' She grinned, an impish little grin that had him groaning inwardly.

A loud noise cracked through the night, ripping Arnav from the dreams that plagued him endlessly, both awake and asleep. Seeing her in the kitchen in those damn shorts again was probably what brought those dreams on.

Letting his head fall back in defeat, he snorted. Who was he kidding? Everything brought it all back. Scrubbing a hand across his eyes, he desperately wished he could rid himself of the temptation that had come knocking at his door.

Noises outside his bedroom door had him stirring himself to investigate. Pulling on a pair of track pants, he opened the door and walked right into family drama. His father and brother were practically nose to nose in the corridor and in the middle of what looked like a furious argument.

Sighing, he wondered if he could just shut the door and go back to sleep. When both of them turned towards him and glared, he knew it would be impossible to do so. With an irate wave of his hand, their father turned from them and walked away without saying a word.

'Trouble in business paradise?' he asked his brother, who still stood there. With his hair standing up in spikes and sleep wrinkles creasing his cheek, it was obvious that daddy dearest had dragged him out of bed.

'Someone killed themselves in one of the rooms at the Cochin hotel.' Knuckling his eyes in a gesture that took Arnav back to their childhood for a moment, Arvin said, 'Cops and press are swarming the place.'

'Why is Dad yelling at you? That can hardly be your fault.'

'Everything can be my fault.' Glancing in the direction their father had disappeared into, he asked, 'Want a drink?'

It was almost four in the morning, but looking at his brother's expression, he knew answering that with an 'I'd rather sleep' was not an option.

'Sure.' Stepping out of the room, he said, 'I think I saw some beer in the fridge earlier.'

'Let's go to my room. I have some stuff in the fridge there.' Arvin was already walking towards the stairs, confident his brother would follow.

'Won't the noise wake up Ananya?'

'So?' With a casual shrug, he dismissed any inconvenience his wife might face from their early morning drinking session.

Resigning himself to more awkwardness, Arnav followed.

∽

Ananya came awake to the sound of masculine voices. Recognizing both, she stayed in bed. Cowardice had never been part of her makeup, but she was tired, so tired of all the pretense, the unpleasantness, the unhappiness. She wanted to close her eyes and wish all of it away, and wake up six years earlier, when she had not met either of the Saxena brothers. She wished she could wake up as Ananya Shastry, not Ananya Saxena. The former had dreams, friends, optimism and a full life. The latter had nothing. The latter *was* nothing.

No, that wasn't true. She wiped away a tear that escaped her ferocious control. She did have her work, which meant the world to her. She was damned if she would let Arvin take that away from her. Sitting up, she turned on the night lamp, picked up her laptop from the side table and buried herself in work.

A sliver of light appeared from under the closed bedroom door. Forcing himself to not think about what it meant, Arnav tried to concentrate on his brother's ramblings. *Ananya in shorts and a tank top. Ananya in bed. Ananya, sleep rumpled and loose-limbed.*

Shit. Whiskey sloshed over the side of his glass and onto the floor. He put the glass he was pretending to drink from on the table in front of him. Unable to find a napkin or tissue anywhere around, he just sucked up whatever had spilled on to his hand. He looked up, his hand still in his mouth, and froze.

There she was. In those damn shorts. Barefoot and tumbled hair. Biting back a curse, he muttered a greeting.

'Well, well, well. Look who's up!' Arvin's sardonic voice cut off anything else he might have said. 'My wonderful wife.'

'I needed my laptop charger.' She avoided Arnav's eyes as she walked past them to the cabinet against the wall. She bent over to access the bottom drawer and had him biting back a curse. He decided the antique-looking clock on the other wall deserved all his attention. It was almost six in the morning and his brother didn't show any signs of winding down.

A loud smack had him snapping his head around. Ananya straightened, an embarrassed flush staining her cheeks. At first glance, it looked like his brother had just smacked her bottom, but Arnav found it hard to believe his brother could be quite that crass.

'What?' Arvin laughed at the look on Arnav's face. 'She's my wife and plus she was asking for it, bending over like that.'

'*She* was getting her laptop's charger,' Ananya said, her cool tone at odds with her heightened colour. 'I'm going to get some work done in the bedroom before I leave for office. You boys enjoy your early morning drinking session.' With one last scathing look, she left the room.

'What the hell is wrong with you?' The words burst out of Arnav's mouth before he could try censoring them.

Arvin shrugged. 'What?'

'What do you mean by "what"? You don't treat your wife, or anyone for that matter, with that kind of disrespect, especially when there is someone else in the room.'

'You're not someone else. You're more than that, aren't you?'

Arnav's blood chilled at the words. *Did Arvin know? He couldn't possibly know unless Ananya had told him.*

'You're my brother.' Relief flooded Arnav at those words. Arvin put his glass down. 'I don't see any need to be anyone but myself in front of my family.'

Reaching down, he removed his prosthetic and leaned it against the table next to him. It still gave Arnav a shock when he saw the stump of what was left of his brother's leg. Arvin had learned to walk with barely any sign of the trauma he'd gone through. There was a fierce determination in him to regain his life after the accident that had almost taken it away. If one didn't know he had an artificial leg, they'd never be able to guess it, thanks to his confident stride. Arnav had tremendous respect for what his brother had achieved in the face of such terrible odds.

Casually pinning up the loose flap of his pyjama leg to the waist band of his pyjamas, Arvin picked up his glass again. Raising it in a toast, he said, 'To the Saxena brothers!'

Arnav took a small sip from his glass. The whiskey burned a fiery trail down his throat.

Tipping his glass at him again, Arvin added, 'To surviving our father.'

That was a toast Arnav could get behind. He let the topic

veer off from Arvin's unacceptable behaviour with Ananya to what a nightmarish experience it was working with their father. He went with the flow, agreeing with whatever Arvin was saying, letting his brother's voice wash over him. It didn't take long before Arvin's words started to merge with each other and he slumped back in his seat.

'He hates me,' his brother slurred.

'No, you're the favourite son,' Arnav corrected him.

'No,' Arvin said. 'You're what he wanted. I'm the spare he got stuck with.'

Arnav shook his head only to realize his brother was no longer paying attention. His head lolled back and a gentle snore escaped him. Sighing, Arnav got to his feet and helped Arvin recline on the couch he was slumped on. Making sure Arvin was comfortable, he tucked a cushion beneath his neck, so he didn't wake up with a crick in it. He straightened and picked up the glasses and the almost empty bottle of Scotch.

'Slut.' The word had him spinning on his heel. But realizing that Arvin was probably mumbling in his sleep, he moved to gently stop his body from rolling off the couch.

'Stupid, fucking slut.' The words were softer now, but still audible. A heightened sense of awareness had Arnav looking up. Ananya met his eyes from across the room.

'I'll handle him from here.' She came forward into the room. 'Thank you.'

The dismissive look she flashed rankled his pride, but he stepped back and let her drape a blanket around Arvin. He watched her pick up Arvin's phone and set an alarm on it before leaving it within easy reach of his arm.

'Does he always talk to you like that?'

Arnav's low voice right behind her had her almost jumping

out of her skin, but years of living with Arvin had taught her how to mask her emotions.

'I'm not sure what you mean.' The cold tone didn't deter him for an instant.

'You think being called a slut is acceptable?'

'How come you're so sure that I'm the one he's calling a slut?' she shot back.

'He slapped your bottom in front of me.'

Her cheeks flushed again at the reminder of that humiliating moment. 'It was a joke.' Ignoring the incredulous look he gave her, she gritted her teeth and said, 'A private joke. I wouldn't expect you to understand.'

When Arnav started to speak again, she held up a hand to stop him.

'I don't appreciate you interfering between my husband and me.' Subtly emphasizing the word 'husband', she added, 'You're here on a holiday to spend time with your family. I suggest you do that and only that. Anything else is none of your business.'

They stared at each other for an endless moment that left Ananya's nerves stretched to a breaking point. Finally, Arnav murmured, 'If that's what you want.'

'It's all I want,' she confirmed.

Stepping around him, she slung her office bag onto her shoulder and left without another word and before he could spot her trembling fingers.

Chapter 4

'A chef?' His father looked up from the newspaper. 'What do you mean you want to be a chef?'

'I want to train in the kitchens, starting from the bottom and—'

'Why don't you just say you want to be someone's wife?' The derisive question silenced Arnav's carefully prepared speech.

'A lot of well-known chefs are men,' he said stiffly.

'I'm offering you a chain of luxury hotels to run and you want to scrub potatoes in a kitchen?'

'Dad, I—'

'Enough!' The paper was slammed against the dining table with enough force to send cutlery clattering to the ground.

'No son of mine is going to be a bloody cook.' The furious roar had attracted the attention of the rest of the household. His mother came running in, followed by Arvin, who kept a safe distance from the unfolding drama.

'Then I guess I'm no son of yours.' The words dropped into the ensuing silence like stones.

For a moment, his father looked too dumbfounded to react. No one had ever refused to back down in front of him.

Quickly recovering, he sneered, 'You bloody fool! You think you can walk out of here and become this magical success story that will show me up?'

'I don't want to do anything of the sort,' Arnav answered. 'I just want to live my life.'

'In the bloody kitchen?'

'Yes, in the bloody kitchen,' Arnav yelled.

The room held its collective breath. No one had shouted at Akhilesh Saxena before and gotten away with it. No one.

His father looked like he was on the verge of an apoplexy. A vein thrummed ominously at his temple even as his hands clenched into fists on either side of his rigid body.

'You won't get anything from me.'

'I'm not asking for anything.' Arnav's tired whisper carried more weight than his father's venomous words. 'I'm just asking for my life, so I can live it the way I want to.'

'Fine.' The sudden capitulation had Arnav glancing at his father warily. 'You want your life? You got it.' Before Arnav could respond, he continued, 'It's all you'll get from me. Now take it and get out.' Arnav was still trying to process his father's words when he shouted, 'Get out. Get out and don't you ever come back. Not when I'm alive and definitely not when I'm dead.'

5

'You really want to buy this dump?' Arvin asked, looking at the dusty, grimy room.

Arnav didn't see what his brother saw. What he saw was the café of his dreams with white wicker furniture and brightly patterned cushions. He saw the brick accent wall with a fireplace that would come alive in the bitter winters that Delhi was famous for. Dramatic landscapes were framed and hung in strategic spots. And most importantly, there was an open kitchen walled in only by glass on one side. He could imagine that space bustling with activity and redolent with the aroma of incredible cooking.

Yes, he really wanted to buy this dump. Grinning, Arnav pushed through the doors at the end and walked towards what would be his dream kitchen some day. The walls and floor were filthy and some of the oily grime stuck to the soles of their shoes. His smile widened as he listened to his brother squelching along and cursing.

'You can wait in the car if you want,' he suggested.

'I don't think my car is even going to be there when we go back out,' Arvin groused. 'Why the hell do you want to open a restaurant in this shithole of a neighbourhood anyway?'

'Café,' Arnav corrected. 'A niche coffee shop that will be both a hangout joint and the perfect spot for a casual date.' It was a perfectly respectable middle-class neighbourhood, maybe beneath his brother's standards but perfectly in line with his own.

'Fine. Whatever.' Arvin dismissed his dream with a wave of his hand. 'Why here?'

Because even the so-called middle-class folks like a nice place to eat at. His brother seemed to have lost sight of that simple fact. His family was so focussed on catering to the higher echelons of society that they considered someone even slightly below their income level an unsavoury target market. He wondered if they even realized to what extent his own ideologies resonated with the ethos of the middle class.

'Are we done here?' With another impatient glance around the place, Arvin started to move towards the door.

Arnav followed him more slowly. He needed to speak with his lawyer and have him scan the property documents at the earliest.

They didn't speak again until they were back in the car. Arvin sat behind the wheel of the German-made luxury ride. 'If this was what you wanted, why didn't you just join the family business?'

Arvin's question jolted Arnav out of his mental calculations. Shoving aside all thoughts of EMIs and interest rates, he answered, 'Because joining the business would be joining Dad.'

'Good point,' Arvin conceded with a bitter twist to his lips.

'Plus, I love cooking and feeding people. Working with a small team at a small café where I can experiment with the menu and interact with the customers is my dream, not running a chain of hotels where the person I see most often is my secretary.'

'Or Dad,' Arvin reminded him. 'I honestly think I see his face even in my dreams.'

Staring out of the window, Arnav relived the day he had told his father about his future plans. The blaring horn of a lorry overtaking them jolted Arnav back to the present. He'd come back for his mother this time even though his father had explicitly banned him from coming back to the house, a fact that his father and he both ignored for the sake of the woman they both loved.

He had come back after managing to find moderate success, a fact that was somewhat palatable to his father. His café, Coffee, Tea, or Me, was a success in the bylanes of Juhu, Mumbai. It was no chain of five-star hotels, but it had one edge over them. It was his.

Sweat, blood and tears, he'd shed them all for his dream, and yes, he'd scrubbed potatoes, along with pots and pans, to get to where he was today. Starting as a mere assistant in the café's kitchen, he'd put in his time for four years until the head chef quit in a temperamental huff.

The owner, whose arrogance rivalled Arnav's father's, had thrown the chef's discarded apron at him and said, 'I bet you can do his job better than him.' And he had.

Recognizing the chance that fate had thrown his way and determined to make the most of it, he had put his head down, unleashed his passion for cooking and worked his fingers to the bone. Both the owner and he were equally astounded by the results. They'd taken the tiny café and turned it into the coolest hangout place in Juhu.

When the owner died of a heart attack and his son, who lived in the US, offered Arnav the option of buying the place, he had mortgaged everything he had, including what felt like a sizeable chunk of his soul, and bought it. The first time he had balanced his books and found the figures in the black, he'd put his head down on the table and wept like a baby.

And soon there would be another café. This time in Delhi. In his father's backyard. It felt right. Finally, his moment had come.

∽

'Papa?' Her father was the last person she'd expected to call her. 'Is everything okay?'

'No, everything isn't okay. Where is your husband?' The irate question had her pulling the car over to the roadside. So this was, as always, related to work. As the head of the law firm that represented the Ariaa Group of Hotels amongst a host of other clients, her father was a busy man. She'd rarely seen him without an appointment.

After checking she had parked carefully, she answered, 'I don't know. Why? Is something wrong?'

'I need to talk to him about the man who died in the Cochin hotel.'

'Someone died?' Her voice rose a couple of octaves. 'How?'

'You don't know?' her father snapped back. 'What kind of marriages do you youngsters have nowadays? Nobody even talks to each other. All the time buried in your laptops and smartphones.'

The irony of the reprimand almost had Ananya smiling. Her only memory of her parent's conversations was of her mother asking her father, 'What do you want for dinner?'

His response would be, 'Nothing. I'll be late. *Office mein khake aa jaaonga* (Will come after eating in office).'

And that would be that, until the next morning, when she would ask him the same question and get the same answer.

Wisely swallowing a retort, Ananya murmured, 'I'll ask him to call you.'

'Don't bother. I can see his call coming through.' With that, he clicked off. Ananya spent an extra moment listening to the disconnected tone before she shoved the phone into her purse and put the car in gear.

That little chat summed up an entire month's worth of conversation with her father. She was surprised he even had her number on his phone. They usually communicated by passing messages through her mother.

Mind still on her father's call, she turned into the driveway.

Her heart sank when she saw Arvin's car in the rearview mirror, pulling in right behind her. Another quick glance told her it was double trouble. Arnav was in the passenger seat. Checking her face to make sure no hint of her inner turmoil showed on it, she grabbed her laptop bag and got out.

'Hello sweetheart.' Wrapping an arm around her, Arvin pulled her stiff body into a hug. 'You're home early.'

Only her husband could make an endearment sound so insulting, she reflected. With Arnav's silence a searing brand on her consciousness, she murmured, 'So are you.'

'Brother bonding time. Arnav is buying a property here. We went to look at that.' On that ominous note, he strode ahead yelling for one of the househelps to take his bag.

'Here?' The word stuck in her throat. 'You can't buy property here!'

She sounded hysterical, but she couldn't help herself.

'I can't?'

She could handle a month of his presence, but if he moved back home... For a moment, Ananya thought she might actually pass out. Arvin had disappeared through the front door and she was left alone with Arnav in the driveway. She took a deep breath and turned to face him.

'Why, Arnav?' For the first time since he'd come home, she let him see the girl he knew. 'Why are you coming home?'

'I'm not. I can never come home again, Anni. You know that.' He kept his voice low, conscious they could be overheard. 'I'm just expanding my business.'

'Expand it somewhere else.' She knew she was being unreasonable, but she didn't care in that moment.

'No.'

The denial was as firm as it was unequivocal. The weight

of it piled on to her already fatigued shoulders. Here was another skein in their tangled web to deal with. For a long moment, they just stared at each other in silence, in pain.

'He's not going to care.' They both knew his father wouldn't care about anything Arnav did. Wanting to display his success in his father's backyard was a futile exercise in hope.

'I know.' He knew it all, but, still, this was something he needed to do. He needed to prove to himself that he could succeed right under his father's nose. He wasn't asking for pride or praise from his father, but even a glimmer of acknowledgement would go a long way.

Ananya saw the hurt he usually kept walled away flash across his face. She raised her hand in an attempt to offer comfort, but reality surfaced and had her curling it at her side. Turning from him, she faced the house before saying, 'We should go in. Arvin will be wondering what's taking us so long.'

In silent agreement, he started forward. They made it to the front door in silence, a silence that screamed a hundred accusations and whispered a million pleas.

Ananya flipped her sunglasses down from their customary spot on her head. She didn't want anyone to catch a glimpse of the turmoil swirling through her. She walked away from Arnav, who had stopped at the foot of the staircase. Taking two stairs at a time, she made it to her bedroom as fast as she could.

She dropped her stuff on the corner chair and rushed to the bathroom. She shut her eyes and splashed water on her overheated face. The cold water was the slap on her face that she needed. Gasping a little, she opened her eyes and found Arvin watching her. Their eyes met in the mirror above the sink.

'Bad day?' He bit into the apple he was holding in his hand as he watched her.

She turned from the sink, water dripping from her chin, but composure back in place.

'Not really,' she replied. 'Arvin—'

But he had already turned away from her and headed back to the bedroom. Ananya followed.

'When did you want to leave for Singapore?'

'Hmm?' Eyes on the TV, he surfed through the channels.

'Singapore. The trip you wanted me to accompany you on?' Ananya prompted.

'Oh that. It may not happen now. Something came up.'

She tried to control her quick flare of temper.

'When will it happen?'

'Don't know,' he said with a shrug and continued to browse TV shows.

'When were you going to tell me?' The bite in her tone had the corner of his lip lifting in a sardonic smile.

'I'm telling you now.'

Now. A day before she was expecting to leave. Her workload, which included a domestic violence case she felt strongly about, had been reassigned and her boss was now under the impression that she was a rich wife pretending to be a serious professional.

Taking a deep breath that barely did anything to control the rising tide of anger, Ananya turned towards her cupboard. Grabbing her gym pants and a tank top, she changed as quickly as she could and left. At best, the space and time would give her a much-needed chance to unleash her fury.

At worst, she'd attempt to outrun her demons.

She ran into one right outside the gate. Ananya groaned when she saw that he, too, was dressed for an evening run.

'Don't...' she snapped, 'don't follow me.'

'I came out the door first,' Arnav pointed out. 'So, technically you followed me.'

She wanted to throw something at his thick head but settled for a glare instead. Turning away from him, she started down the driveway at a pace that would have left a lesser man in the dust. It annoyed her that he not only kept pace with her but didn't seem the least bit winded. They turned on to the tarred road outside in perfect harmony. Ananya felt her mood sour further.

'Can't you find somewhere else to run?' she gritted out.

'If we run together, you can run further.'

She couldn't dispute his words for the sheer sense it made. She usually stuck to the main road right in front of their house in a bid to stay as safe as possible. A girl running alone at this time of the day was a prime target for all the riffraff in town. If she stayed in sight of the security manning their gates, she knew no one would misbehave with her. However, that would mean pretty much running laps on the same road in front of the house.

Arnav's presence by her side meant that she could venture further. The thought brought with it a whiff of freedom that was like balm to her bruised soul. She didn't need to stay in sight of the house, like a dog on a leash.

With that in mind, she pushed for a burst of speed that took Arnav by surprise. It didn't take long for him to catch up, a fact that still irritated her for no reason. They ran in silence, each lost in their own thoughts.

Reaching a small park, they passed through the metal gate and took to the joggers' path that ran around its circumference. Ananya let the stress and pain that had taken up permanent residence in her mind fade away for a brief while.

She concentrated on each breath that puffed out from between her lips, every twinge of muscle with her lengthening stride, every rapid thump of her heart as it pounded to keep up. For the first time in years, she forgot about the hell she woke up in, the hell she lived in, the hell she survived. She forgot everything, even her past, though it ran beside her with a silent, lethal grace. She forgot it all for the moment.

A sudden shout brought her out of her trance and back to the world around her. She kept one eye trained on the drama unfolding near the gate even as she continued to run with the easy, loping stride that had won her every track event she had ever participated in. By her side, Arnav continued to run in silence.

The argument at the other end of the track looked like it was dying down, at least on the surface. The man turned away from the woman and could be seen helping himself to a serving of chaat at the roadside stall next to them. Something about him held Ananya's gaze even as she took the final turn that led to the gate. A split second later, he spun around again, the plate of chaat flying in the poor woman's face.

Ananya was already skidding to a stop near them even before the woman's first shriek filled the air. With the curd, chutney, sev, puris and all the other accompaniments dripping from her face, she continued to cry loudly even as Ananya stepped between them. She grabbed the man's raised hand stopping its forward arc.

'Don't.' They looked affluent enough to understand English, but she was more than willing to switch to Hindi if need be. Holding the man's aggressive stare even as he jerked his hand out of her grasp, she asked the lady weeping behind her, 'Are you okay?'

'*Ji.*' The sobs trailed into whimpers and hiccups.

Arnav stood shoulder to shoulder with her in a show of silent support that she resented as much as she appreciated. The man's aggressive stance wilted a bit as a fairly large crowd gathered around them.

'*Chalo.*' The curt command had the woman still standing behind Ananya coming forward hesitantly.

'*Ek second.*' Ananya's clear voice halted the woman's progress and she turned to face her. Taking the woman's phone from her tightly clenched fingers, Ananya quickly punched in her contact number.

'*Lawyer hoon. Madad chahiye toh phone karna* (I am a lawyer. If you need help, call me).' She threw a stern look at the outraged husband, who looked like he wanted to raise his hand again, except in Ananya's direction this time.

Arnav shifted towards Ananya, a move that told her he was ready to intervene if required. Surprised he hadn't tried to pull her away already and more than a little grateful that he hadn't undermined her in that way, she handed the phone back to the still trembling woman.

'*Nahin, didi. Sab theek hain* (No, everything is alright),' she spoke through her tears.

She could still hear the man berating his wife in an angry undertone as they moved away from them. The crowd started to disperse looking more than a little disappointed that there had been no drama to entertain them. Within seconds, Arnav and Ananya were standing alone even as the chaat vendor grumbled in the background, looking at his wasted dish now smashed into the dirt.

'Well, that was phenomenally stupid.' The low growl almost made her jump.

With the poised mask which she had carefully cultivated over the years of her marriage firmly in place, she turned to face the furious man standing behind her.

'I beg your pardon?'

'What the hell do you think you were doing?'

She was surprised he managed to get the words out through that viciously clenched jaw. About to snap back at him, she remembered that he'd waited. He hadn't interfered or yelled at her during...

'I was trying to help.' She turned away from him and started walking towards home.

'You just gave a complete stranger your private number. That stranger is married to a man who looked more than prepared to smack you in the face just now. I ask again, what the hell were you thinking?'

'She needed help and I was in a position to offer it. And in my line of work, all the women who have my number have spouses and family who hate my guts. It comes with the job.'

He dogged her heels as she calmly crossed the road and stopped to buy a bottle of mineral water from a small grocery store.

'Thank you, bhaiya.' Smiling, she paid up and continued to walk.

'Water?' She offered the bottle to him. When he did nothing but stare at her, she shrugged and continued walking down the road. Taking a large sip, she let the cold water trickle down her throat and cool her overheated body.

'Have you lost your mind, Anni?'

And just like that all goodwill evaporated. She stopped while they were still out of earshot of the guard who stood at their gate.

'I've told you NOT to call me that.'

'That's what you're going to argue with me about?' He was furious. 'You of all people should know how unsafe this city can be. You put yourself in danger for no reason and—'

'I had the biggest possible reason,' Ananya interrupted. 'That woman needed help.'

'She didn't ask for your help. In fact, she pretty much told you to mind your own business.'

'Not everyone can ask for help.' With anger, guilt and hurt swirling in a vitriolic mix inside her, Ananya shot back, 'Sometimes, you need to hear the cries in their silence.'

Her words seemed to have a bulb light up in his head.

'No. God, no.' The anguished whisper tore at her heart. 'Please tell me my brother doesn't abuse you. If he does—'

'Your brother,' she forced the words out through her numb lips, praying he wouldn't pick up on the distinction she made, 'has never raised his hands on me, not once.'

He instinctively reached for her. 'Then why put yourself at any personal risk, Anni—'

'Don't. Call. Me. That.' The words sliced through the air and had him dropping the hand he'd extended.

'Why?' He shoved his hands into his pockets, so he didn't make the same mistake again.

'Anni doesn't exist. Not anymore. It is only Ananya now.' Ananya did not merely exist. She survived. She had built a life, brick by brick, on the shattered remnants of Anni. But that wasn't something she was going to share with the man standing across from her, the man whose love both defined and destroyed her.

Chapter 5

'We have to stop running into each other like this.'

Arnav turned from the railing to see Ananya step onto the terrace. She looked startlingly lovely in a cream-coloured ghaghra choli that revealed more than it covered.

'Cigarette?' He held out his open pack, but she shook her head.

'I'm trying to keep my promise.'

Arnav raised his eyebrows. 'Bravo.'

'Trying,' she said, rubbing her hands against her arms in a vain bid to warm herself. 'Let's see what comes of it.'

'You know what would warm you up?' Arnav asked. 'More fabric.'

Ananya looked askance at the jeans, T-shirt and jacket he was wearing. Even in the semi darkness, he knew they looked old and faded.

'I don't think you should be giving me fashion advice.'

'True.' He took a deep drag of his cigarette. 'But I'm warm.'

She laughed, the sound as always going straight to his gut.

'True,' she repeated.

Arnav watched her as she stepped up to stand by his side. Taking off his jacket, he draped it around her shoulders without a word. Ananya smiled in gratitude and slid her hands into the warmth of the pockets.

Shoulder to shoulder, they looked down at the party organized in the lawns.

'Why are you out here if not for a cigarette? Shouldn't the bride-to-be stay down there, smiling prettily and mingling with everyone?'

She didn't answer. They stood in silence looking down at the glittery, glamorous crowd milling around like sheep.

'Can I ask you something?'

'Sure,' he answered, without thinking.

'Why doesn't your brother find me attractive?' she blurted out.

Arnav gaped at her, his cigarette dangling limply from his fingers. 'What?'

'He doesn't touch me.' Now that she'd started, Ananya couldn't stop the words from spilling out of her mouth. With the dam broken, the words burst out of her. 'He doesn't hold me, kiss me...he doesn't seem to want to.'

Arnav was horrified to realize that for the first time in his life, he was blushing! Cheeks flaming, he cleared his throat and tried to think of something to say. But, for the life of him, he could not come up with anything.

'It can't be normal, can it?' Ananya bit her lower lip and stared at the huge number of people gathered to celebrate her upcoming nuptials. 'That he doesn't want to...'

Her voice trailed off, leaving them standing next to each other in excruciatingly embarrassing silence.

Arnav still had nothing that he could think of to say. His mind was completely blank.

'I'm not a gargoyle,' she muttered now. Shucking off his jacket, she spread her hands to the side and gestured to herself. 'Am I?'

Arnav looked at her. Her every curve was silhouetted by the lights that shone behind her. She looked incredible. Svelte, sexy, attractive and completely out of his reach.

'Yes,' he finally managed to say. 'You are.'

'A gargoyle?' Ananya gaped at him disbelievingly. After a startled pause, she burst into laughter. Tears ran down her cheeks as she laughed. 'Serves me right. Serves me right for asking that question.'

'A very beautiful gargoyle,' he said huskily.

The words stopped her laughter in a heartbeat. They stared at each other in the shadows, the loud sounds and bright lights of the party barely reaching where they stood.

'If we were engaged, would you have—'

'No,' he replied, not waiting for her to finish the question, not wanting her to finish. 'I'm not a patient man.'

'There's something terribly wrong with the fact that he is.' Her words were softer than a whisper, if that was possible.

'Talk to him,' he advised, even as pain knotted his gut. 'Tell him this bothers you.'

'I have.' Ananya turned to face him. 'He says there's no time. Had it been us, would you not have had the time to kiss me, to touch me, to make me feel—' She stopped talking abruptly, her face flushed.

Arnav thought his head would explode at her words. 'Anni, there is no us.'

'Anni.' She smiled as she said, 'I like it when you call me that. I've never been an Anni to anyone before.'

'Ananya,' he said as repressively as he could manage, 'this is a ridiculous conversation.'

Her smile faded at his choice of words. 'Ridiculous?'

'Yes. You are marrying my brother in three weeks. This is a conversation you should be having with him and not with me.'

She took a deep breath and stepped back.

'This is...' He searched for the right word and found it. *'Inappropriate.'*

Ananya flinched. She picked up the jacket she'd shrugged off earlier and handed it to him. 'I should leave.'

'Yes.' He stepped aside and let her pass.

Her hand brushed against his in passing and he curled his fingers into a fist. The barest caress of her skin against his and his fingers trembled. He was pathetic, a pathetic loser who wanted someone he could never have. Unfortunately, he had just found out that she, too, wanted him.

It changed nothing and changed everything at the same time.

∽

Cooking had helped him stay sane on more occasions than he could count. Knowing the kitchen would be deserted at five in the morning and unable to pretend that he was sleeping any longer, Arnav made his way downstairs.

He opened up the fridge and surveyed the contents. Not finding any meat in the freezer, he frowned and looked in the vegetable basket. A decent assortment of vegetables looked back at him. Grabbing whatever he thought he could manage with, he set to work.

As he chopped and sliced his way through a tiny mountain of vegetables, his mind stayed on the scene from the previous evening. He understood her need to help, but still didn't understand her complete lack of self-preservation. Something niggled at the back of his mind. He felt he was missing something important.

Opening one of the lower cupboards in search of a cooking pot, he almost whacked his head on the open panel when someone spoke from behind him.

'Looking for something to cook in?'

Heavy eyed and with hair that made a bird's nest look good, she looked as fresh as he felt.

'No,' the devil on his shoulder answered. 'I was just trying to make off with some of the ancestral silverware.'

'We don't keep it in the kitchen.' The cold look she gave him had his fingers clenching around the ladle. 'It's in a locked cupboard in the pantry. Want the key?'

He grinned at the barb and only got a bad-tempered scowl in return. Muttering under her breath, she moved past him to put some milk on the stove.

For a while after that there was only silence broken by the clatter of utensils being used. He didn't mind. He was a man used to his own company, and Ananya in the same room as him, even an Ananya who didn't talk, was an unexpected gift.

Half a mug of coffee later, she asked, 'What are you making?'

'Mixed vegetable stew.' Turning from the stove to face her, he said, 'I thought I'd make some appams to go with it for breakfast.'

There was no answer, just another big gulp of coffee. Shrugging, he moved to rinse his hands in the sink.

'Anni.'

She slammed her mug down on the table.

'Ananya,' he corrected himself before she got more pissed off. She was right. Anni, *his* Anni, didn't exist anymore. In front of him was Arvin's Ananya, and he owed it to both his brother and his brother's wife to not cause any conflict during his short stay with them.

His heart felt like a raw bruise in his chest as he sat down across from her.

'Ananya,' he repeated, 'why are you awake at this godforsaken hour?'

For a moment there he thought she wouldn't answer. But she did. 'It's easier to be up and about than to lie in bed staring at the ceiling.'

The shadows in her eyes made him itch to reach for her, but he kept his hands at his side and waited.

'Why are you cooking at this hour?' she finally asked.

'It relaxes me.' The non-controversial answer had her shoulders relaxing. 'Every self-respecting chef starts his day early.'

'You're not a chef anymore.' She took another small sip from her mug. 'You're a very successful business owner, a king of your own little fiefdom.'

'Aww shucks.' Giving her his best attempt at a bashful smile, he said, 'I'd hardly call myself that.'

A faint smile tugged at her lips. 'What would you call yourself?'

He pretended to think about it. 'His Royal Awesomeness.'

Ananya laughed. The sound of her laughter caused his heart to stutter a bit before settling again. Maybe he had inherited his mother's mythical heart ailment.

'It's the first time I've heard you laugh since I've come back.' The words escaped him before he could swallow them unsaid. 'You should laugh more.'

Her smile faded as she watched him. A wealth of grief darkened those eyes that had always seemed to look straight into his soul.

'Can I taste it?' she asked, tilting her head towards the bubbling stew.

'I'll fix you a plate for a price.' He smiled, hoping to bring her smile back.

He was rewarded with a faint glimmer of one.

'What do you want?'

Getting up, he ladled some stew into a bowl and grabbed a spoon. 'Answers.'

When she didn't reply immediately, he added, 'A harmless conversation. Nothing more, nothing less.'

He kept his back to her as he searched through the kitchen cabinets for a wok. Silence reigned. Unable to take it anymore, he decided to change the topic. 'I soaked the rice last night, so this should come out well.'

He'd poured a spoonful of appam batter into the wok when she finally spoke, 'I, too, get to ask questions.'

His hand froze midair, right above the frying appam.

'I'm sorry?' Not sure he'd heard right, he turned to face her.

Bringing her mug to her lips, she took another sip before saying, 'I'll make a pact with you. For every question I answer, I get to ask you one.'

'Deal.' He grinned. Just when he was about to say something more, the smell of something burning had him spinning back to the stove. Ananya laughed as he cursed, taking in the sight of the burnt appam—so much for his reputation as a hotshot chef.

Pouring another spoonful, he waited for the appam to rise beautifully before he scooped it out. Setting the meal before her, he asked, 'How many more?'

'Just this one is more than enough. Thank you.'

He frowned. 'Are you dieting or something?' She was already skin and bones.

'No. Just not used to eating so early in the morning.'

'Okay.' Sitting down opposite her, he said, 'So—'

'Uh huh.' Ananya shook her head. 'My turn now.'

She was in a playful mood. He was delighted to see her past self returning, the one he knew. 'That was not a legit question. I was just asking you if you wanted another appam.' He feigned outrage but sat back in surrender. 'Fine. Go ahead.'

'Was it worth it?'

His heart knew what she was asking, but he still pretended to be puzzled. 'Was what worth it?'

'Leaving home, leaving the family, striking out on your own?'

'Yes.' The answer to that question was a simple one. 'I have some regrets in life, but striking out on my own will never be one of them.'

It was his turn now. Determined to keep the conversation generic and harmless, he asked, 'Have you ever thought of starting your own law firm?'

'No.' Her reply was quick, almost like she didn't need to think about it. 'I like my firm and the people who work there. Most importantly, I'm proud of the work and the results we, as a team, achieve there. I doubt I'd be as effective on my own.'

Acknowledging her response with a nod, he inclined his head and waited for her to ask him something.

'What has been your most terrifying moment in the last few years?'

He laughed. 'The day I signed the bank loan to buy my café. My fingers were shaking terribly. I didn't think the bank would accept my wonky signature. It was both the most exhilarating and the most terrifying moment of my life.

'What do you consider your biggest win?' he asked her now.

Arnav watched as she mulled over his question. The squiggly lines marring her otherwise smooth forehead, the tiny nose turned up in thought—all of that seemed adorable to him. Slamming the brakes on that thought, he waited for her to answer.

'There was this woman who walked into our office one day claiming she was being abused by her in-laws. Long story short, she cited several examples of dowry harassment, physical and mental torture. She even pulled back the sleeve of her dress and showed us cigarette burn marks on both hands. Her husband, according to her, liked using her as an ashtray and kept stubbing out his cigarettes on her.'

Arnav listened in silence. The world could be a horrible place and unfortunate as it was, stories like these were far more common than one could imagine.

'My boss assigned me to do due diligence on the case and the file landed on my desk with all the resulting paperwork. I met her on several occasions, but there was something that didn't add up. I had nothing to back up the feeling, but my instinct told me there was something I was missing. I knew where her husband worked, so I pretended to bump into him at a coffee shop near his office. We chatted, mostly small talk, as we stood in the queue to place our orders. The minute I stood close to him, I knew what it was that had been bugging me.'

The animation in her face took his breath away. He didn't realize until that moment that he hadn't seen it at all since he'd come home. She'd been like a robot on auto pilot, until now.

'Smokers stink.'

Arnav choked on the sip of coffee he'd been quietly sneaking from her mug without her knowledge. As a smoker himself, he was more than a little offended. And as someone who had quit smoking, she didn't seem to realize she had just dissed them both.

'Excuse me?'

'You know what they say.' She waved a hand in the air. 'Kissing a smoker is like licking an ashtray.'

His mouth fell open, but Ananya didn't notice. She was too caught up in her story. Spooning in a mouthful of stew, she stopped for a moment. 'This is delicious. No wonder your café is such a massive success.'

Still annoyed by the dirty ashtray comparison, he gave her a curt nod in acknowledgement of the praise and said, 'So, he stank?'

'No,' Ananya said, excitement seeping into her voice. 'He didn't.'

'Then?' Arnav frowned.

'She did.' Ananya did a little bounce and wiggle in her seat, which did strange things to his anatomy. He ordered his ashtray lips to behave.

'Ahh.' He could see where this was going. 'I would have thought your big win would have been helping a woman who was being abused.'

'It's never been about men and women for me,' she answered. 'It's about right and wrong, helping the victims find their voice, being the light that guides people who've lost all hope of finding their way out of a desperate situation. It is, as clichéd as it sounds, about justice.' Ananya stopped abruptly. She looked a little embarrassed by her sudden speech. 'I didn't mean to get up on my soapbox. Sorry.'

'Don't be.' Warmth wove through his words. 'Hearing that was worth my time slaving over a hot stove.'

Ananya laughed. She gestured to her bowl of stew with her spoon. 'This is probably what food in heaven tastes like. I wish I could cook like this.'

'I'm sure you're not too bad,' Arnav said with a smile.

'The first time I cooked for your parents after the wedding, I gave them a mild bout of food poisoning.'

Arnav froze, the mug of coffee halfway to his lips. 'You didn't!'

'I did.' She nodded, emphatically. 'I believe your father was in the toilet for the better half of that day.'

He tried, he really did, but nothing could stop him from laughing. Collapsing in his seat, he held on to his hurting sides at the thought of his father with all his dignity and pomp running for the toilet after eating the first meal cooked by the daughter-in-law of the family. Tears ran down his cheeks. He couldn't stop laughing like a loon.

'Don't laugh. It was mortifying.' Ananya protested even as chuckles escaped her.

'You're a riot. God, Anni. I've missed you so damn much.' He couldn't stop those words from escaping. Hoping he hadn't ruined the moment, he looked at her to find her still smiling at him.

His gaze warmed her within. It lit the cold embers of the person she'd once been, the person she'd been with him long ago. It had been so long since someone had looked at her the way he did now, like she was someone worth looking at, someone worth knowing, someone worth loving. She hated that the warmth of his gaze made her want to curl up like a puppy basking in the sun.

'I've missed you, too.' The whispered words landed in the quiet kitchen like an activated grenade. Their gazes caught and meshed, mute emotion bubbling between them. A thousand words unspoken, a million questions unanswered.

'Anni.'

Ananya closed her eyes on the husky whisper. How many times had he called her by that name? Unvoiced longing leapt up and clogged her throat while hot tears burned the back of her eyes. Her hand clenched around the spoon she still held. His broad, calloused hand lay inches away from hers. All she had to do was extend her hand a little, reach out and hold on to his.

Forcing her fingers to unclench, she drew back. Those few inches may as well have been the width of a continent. She would never reach out. She couldn't. Pushing her chair back, she stepped away from the table.

'Thank you for the food.' They both pretended to ignore her trembling voice.

'Thank you for the memory. I'll always treasure it.'

Tears sprang to Ananya's eyes at the unvarnished emotion in his voice. They stared at each other for an endless moment, before stepping back from each other.

Hard as it was, Ananya turned from him and walked away. After all, she'd done it before, too.

∽

The warmth of the time she'd spent with Arnav had a thin crack snaking through the ice that encased her heart nowadays. Hugging the memory, she felt the glow from those precious moments heal some of the fractures inside her. Humming softly to herself, she entered her bedroom and came to an abrupt halt.

Arvin sat, propped up in bed, waiting for her.

'Where were you?' The quiet tone didn't fool her. A closer look and she spotted the fine lines that fanned out from his eyes and the tight cast of his lips. He was in pain. And when Arvin was in pain, Ananya suffered.

'I couldn't sleep, so I went to get some coffee.' She tried to keep her tone casual. 'How come you're awake?'

'I couldn't sleep either.' Nightmares. His life was just one endless nightmare. Bitterness tightened its grip around his heart. 'Come in and close the door, Ananya.'

Ananya's heart stopped. Her blood turning ice cold and her limbs moving slower than normal, she stepped into the room and did as she was ordered. No questions were asked. The door shut with a resounding click at her back.

'Come here.' He hadn't moved an inch, but his eyes tracked her every movement.

Walking forward, she came to a stop near the bed, out of his reach, but close enough for him not to snap.

'Take off your clothes.'

The tiny flicker of warmth Arnav had brought to life inside her was dead again.

She'd made a promise to herself and to Arvin the day she'd married him. She'd be the best wife, the best partner he could ever ask for. She'd give him whatever he wanted to make him happy, to make up for what she'd taken from him. She kept the promise. Every. Single. Day. It was in moments like these when she realized what that promise had cost her.

Without blinking, she pulled her T-shirt over her head

and stepped out of her shorts. Standing in front of him in just her panties, she waited.

'All your clothes.'

She hooked her fingers into her panties and pulled them down. Straightening, she tossed them in the direction of her other discarded clothes. Naked, she stood, eyes staring at a point over his shoulder.

'Get in bed.'

She climbed in next to him and lay down. The blinding white of the ceiling filled her sight even as goosebumps erupted on her exposed flesh from the blast of the air-conditioned vent right above her.

'Not like that,' he said in a voice devoid of any emotion. 'On your hands and knees.'

Without a word, she complied. Bracing herself on her hands, she waited. A hand landed on her right thigh, pulling it firmly to one side, exposing her further. She maintained the humiliating position without a murmur.

Silence filled the room for excruciating seconds before she heard a rustle behind her. A hard hand reached between her legs, fondling her intimately. His breathing quickened. It was the only sound in the room now. She stayed still, maintaining the position she was in.

One palm pressed down between her shoulder blades pushing her forward on to her chest, leaving her hips raised and tilted further back. Moments later, she felt him push inside her, into her flesh. Neither was there any resistance nor was he welcomed. Closing her eyes, she waited as he moved, slowly at first and then faster.

Something wet trickled down her cheek and reached her lips. Wet and salty. She turned her face into the pillow by her head to hide the evidence of her tears. They were worth nothing and would do her no good.

Flesh slapped into flesh. Harsh smacking sounds and the creaking of the bed filled the room. Her entire body jerked forward with each forceful thrust.

On a hoarse grunt, he finished, his body, a dead weight against her back for seconds, before he rolled away from her. Ananya let her body slump down on the bed, instinctively curling into a fetal position. Another few seconds passed, and she heard him move slowly on one foot to the bathroom. Each pained and shuffling hop was a dagger to her throbbing heart.

Chapter 6

Ananya stared at herself in the mirror. The month-long festivities that were going to culminate in her wedding had started. Tonight, there was an informal dinner party at her future in-laws' house. It was finally happening. She was going to be Mrs Ananya Saxena. Mrs Ananya Arvin Saxena.

She was excited. Of course, she was. Who wouldn't be? Arvin was a catch by pretty much anyone's standards. He was handsome, educated and successful. More importantly, they were friends. They enjoyed each other's company, they respected each other, they valued each other... She sounded like a ninety-year-old woman giving advice to her granddaughter.

It wasn't that she didn't know the importance and value of companionship, friendship, respect and all of that, but was it so very wrong to have hoped for something more? Passion, desire, romance... She had thought it would all eventually happen. Arvin and she liked each other, so there was no reason for it not to...but it hadn't.

Ananya had waited and waited. Their first official date had ended with a polite peck on the lips. She remembered how she had still had her lips pursed, waiting for something more passionate, but Arvin had already been striding off to the car with a casual wave.

The next time he'd called to say he'd pick her up for dinner, she'd amped up her limited assets. Let's face it, no one was going to be calling her buxom or voluptuous. She knew she was adequate at best. But there were the wonders of the push-up bra at play and boy did they push up! She had worn her magic lingerie and waited for Arvin, only to find out he'd come with his mother and aunts in tow. She'd had to hastily grab a shawl to cover up her idiotic display and head out to a family dinner.

They'd played hide and seek like this for what felt like forever before Ananya finally had her moment. Arvin and she went clubbing with their group of friends and ended up drifting slightly away from the rest of the crowd on the dance floor.

Tired from a long day at work, the glass of wine she'd had as soon as they got there had gone straight to her head. Deliciously high on life and happy to finally have a private moment with her fiancé, Ananya dropped all subtleties and grabbed him.

Hands on his lapels, she hauled his surprised face forward and planted a kiss on his lips in the middle of the dance floor. She'd heard the hoots and catcalls from the crowd around them and the muffled curse from Arvin, but what had her rooted to the spot with her arms around the man she was going to spend the rest of her life with was the fact that she felt nothing. Zilch. Nada. No tingle, no squiggle, nothing.

She had never tried pulling another stunt like that. He had muttered an embarrassed 'people are watching' and guided her off the dance floor. He hadn't initiated anything since.

Ananya had always assumed that the passion she wanted would eventually come when the time and the moment would be right. The passion was finally here. It had just come for the wrong man.

∽

Arvin stared at his reflection in the ornate mirror that hung over the bathroom sink. The water he had splashed on his face was dripping from the strands of his hair. Several trickles of it streamed down his cheeks almost like tears. But they weren't. To cry, to shed tears, he would have to feel. And Arvin didn't feel. He hadn't in a very long time.

Why were his hands shaking then? He gripped the counter's edge in a bid to stop the trembling, but it didn't help. When he realized the fine tremors were running through his entire frame, he carefully slid down to the floor. Resting his back against the wall behind him, he waited for it to pass.

Something that felt a lot like disgust moved through him. This was what his life had come to. He was sitting on the bathroom floor with one leg, while his entire body shook like that of a malaria patient.

He stared at the stump that protruded from the bottom of his boxers—a useless and painful reminder of all he had lost. He had lost it all the day he lost her. Arvin closed his eyes and let his head fall back.

He'd loved her once. She had been one of the most important people in his life. They had been friends for years before he had proposed. They fit together perfectly, or so he'd thought. Their ambitions, their wants, their needs had all aligned in almost cosmic harmony. She had said yes. She had been happy. She had been happy to marry him.

Until she'd fallen in love with someone else. He remembered the pain slicing through him when he'd heard her confession, and then it had been followed by months and months of endless, mind-numbing agony that had driven everything else out of his mind.

She'd been there, every single day.

He had shouted at her, ignored her, even had security throw her out once. And still she came back to sit in the single chair positioned by his hospital bed. He had hated every single minute of her presence in that sterile hospital room. Her silent guilt and self-loathing had scraped across his senses like someone was raking him bloody with metal claws.

His rage at her betrayal and his bitter resentment with the circumstances had gotten him through those dark days. He had channelled it all into being mobile again. She had stayed through all of it. He had not wanted her support or her comfort. He sure as hell had not wanted her.

But he did marry her because he loved her. He loved her until he hated her.

∽

Ananya scrubbed her hands over her face, wishing she could wipe out her memories that easily.

'*Didi, aap se milne koi aaya hai* (Madam, someone has come to see you).'

Ananya looked up in acknowledgement of the peon's announcement.

'*Andar bhejo* (Send them inside).' The response was more automatic than conscious. Every inch of her body ached like she'd been beaten black and blue. In her mind she knew it was more about the mental and emotional agony than the physical hurt.

'Madam.'

She looked up at the hesitant greeting. The woman hovering at her door looked vaguely familiar, but she didn't recognize her yet. It took her a moment, but then it came to her. It was the woman from the park. She had gotten in touch with Ananya a few days back and the latter had told her the name of her law firm, so she could come by if she wanted to.

Standing, she gestured to her to come inside and have a seat. Shutting the office door, so no one could listen in on their conversation, she came back to lean against the desk in front of her.

'Tell me.' She spoke in Hindi, sensing the woman was more comfortable with the language.

'You said,' she spoke hesitantly, 'I could come to you if I needed help.'

Listening to someone unburden themselves was often the best support you could offer. Ananya stayed silent as the woman talked. She made notes and plans. She let Payal, as the woman introduced herself, talk until the words that poured out of her initially in a feverish rush slowed to a calmer, more settled pace.

'I was married a day after my eighteenth birthday. My parents waited for me to reach the legal age. They had already chosen my husband, and the discussions and negotiations had been done.'

Negotiations. It was a good word for what went on in arranged marriage scenarios, Ananya reflected.

'I was happy, Madam. Nobody forced me to marry him. He was from a good, affluent family and my parents agreed to the offer. He is a doctor and has a very well-established practice. His entire family is well-educated. I am just a graduate and had no interest in a career, but they didn't care. They liked me. The wedding also happened with minimum drama. My parents gave them everything that they asked for and they were pleased with that.'

Ananya poured a glass of water from the jug she kept handy at all times. She gave Payal the glass and moved to sit behind her desk.

'What happened after you got married?' she asked.

Payal's hand shook, drops of water fell on her chiffon saree.

'Everything changed.' She took a deep breath before continuing, 'Initially, he never paid any attention to me and I used to feel bad about that. I wondered if there was something wrong with me that my husband didn't bother to have any kind of relationship with me. I was a fool.' Tears glimmered in her eyes. 'I should have been grateful for that time when he ignored me.'

Her hand started shaking so badly that she had to put the glass back on the table. Ananya didn't say a word. She waited for Payal to regain her composure and continue.

'About a year into our marriage, one day he came home from a friend's house. He was drunk and angry, I don't know why.' Lost in the memories of that night, she stared into nothingness for a moment.

'How does it even matter anymore?' She shook her head. 'He was angry and I was there, like I always was, ironing his clothes for the next day. It was a white shirt. I remember. He—' she paused, giving Ananya a miserable look. 'Do I have to give you all the details?'

'What do you want to do, Payal? That's the first question we have to answer,' Ananya replied.

'I want...' she hesitated. 'Is it possible to leave him?'

'Are you sure about this?' Ananya asked. 'Have you thought this through? You won't change your mind suddenly?'

'Yes. I am sure.' Fear lit Payal's teary eyes. 'I'm scared. If I stay in this marriage, I am scared that one day it will be too late for me. It's getting worse, Madam. Every day, it's getting worse. Please tell me, is it possible for me to leave him?'

'Yes. It most definitely is,' Ananya answered, decisively. 'And for that I will need details. What did he do that night?'

Payal's gaze dropped to her tightly clenched hands. The knuckles turned white as she continued to twist her slender fingers.

'He pushed me from behind onto the bed.' The words were a bare whisper, but she heard her. For a second, Ananya saw herself pressed face down on the bed, naked, legs spread. Shaking her head to dispel the image, she brought back her focus to Payal.

'He pushed himself into me. Into my bottom. It was so painful I blacked out. I don't remember much more from that night. When I woke up, he was not in the room. Had I not been bleeding, I would have thought I had imagined it all.'

No, you didn't imagine it.

Grimly, Ananya continued to draw Payal's story out of her. It gave her no pleasure to listen to the sad, sordid tale of rape, abuse and pain, but she listened carefully because every detail mattered, every detail would be crucial in Payal's fight for freedom.

'Why now?' she asked when Payal finally came to the end of the story. 'Why have you decided to leave him now after five years of marriage?'

'He wants children.' A shudder ran through her frail

body. 'I can't do it, Madam. I can't have a child with that man. I can't.'

Her rising hysteria had Ananya laying a calming hand on her shoulder.

'Can you help me, Madam? That day near the park, you had said you can help.'

'Yes. I can and I will,' Ananya vowed. She glanced at her notes. 'Shall we begin?'

∽

'Ananya.'

Her boss was beckoning her into an empty conference room. In a red salwar kameez and matching lip colour, she looked like more of a socialite and less of a hard-ass lawyer for the underdog, but Ananya knew different. Her boss, Prachi Sareen, redefined hard-ass, both as a lawyer and as a boss.

Walking in, Ananya took the seat across from her and waited for her to speak.

'The new case,' Prachi started without preamble. 'Brief me.'

Quickly, Ananya ran through the facts of Payal's case. Knowing her boss and her impatience with people who rambled and didn't get to the point, she only highlighted the main points.

'Is this going to be a revenue generator or another one of your bleeding heart projects?'

Ananya kept her face blank. She'd been expecting the brusque question. They may get to fight the good fight in court, but at the end of the day, Prachi had a firm to run. And this case was probably not going to be a huge revenue generator.

'He's a doctor and it's a strong case with plenty of evidence and eyewitnesses.'

'And these eyewitnesses won't disappear just when we need them?'

'No,' Ananya hesitated. 'Although we both know there is never any guarantee in these cases.'

'Will your client change her mind? Decide on a reconciliation?'

Again, Ananya hesitated. Her gut said no, but she knew the myriad pressures that could come to impact Payal's decision.

'The risk is the same as with any other client,' she finally said. She wasn't going to give her boss any false guarantees.

'You approached this woman at a park?' Faint amusement coloured Prachi's tone.

'Her husband threw a plate of sevpuri in her face. It caught my attention,' Ananya retorted.

'I bet it did.' Prachi tapped a pen against the table. 'I don't understand you, Ananya.'

The sudden observation took Ananya by surprise. 'I'm sorry?' She straightened up in her chair, a little surprised. Prachi didn't normally make conversation about anything unrelated to the cases they worked on.

'You're so driven and passionate about the work we do here, and you always fight harder when it comes to domestic violence cases. They seem to strike some kind of chord with you. You're like a dog with a bone. A feral dog at that. And then suddenly out of the blue, you request time off to go on an international holiday with your husband, and that too when some of your cases are at critical junctures. Though I understand you didn't end up going in the end, but you intended to earlier.'

Ananya stayed silent. There was nothing she could say. Her boss was right about everything, be it her passion for her work or her perceived flighty behaviour the previous week. She couldn't offer a defence, so she thought it was best to keep her mouth shut.

Prachi sat back in her chair and studied the younger woman seated across from her. She had class stamped into every pore of her and yet she fought for her clients like a street fighter wrestling in mud.

She was a fascinating contradiction and one that Prachi hadn't been able to make up her mind about. The girl was one of her best employees until she suddenly decided to play wife to her rich husband. Prachi knew about the Saxenas. Everyone did. But Ananya didn't fit into any of the gossip she'd heard about them.

Making up her mind about the decision that had been bothering her, she leaned forward.

'I'm planning to make some structural changes in the firm. I'm no longer able to manage both my caseload, the day-to-day overseeing of the lawyers as well as their cases. I plan to split up the firm based on the work we do. One section will be devoted to the domestic violence cases, one section to the divorce cases we get and the third will focus on drafting wills, business agreements and other corporate paperwork. I'll oversee it all, of course, along with my regular caseload, but the daily supervision will come under senior lawyers who will be reporting to me.'

Ananya nodded. Her heart had started to beat uncomfortably fast. If this conversation was going where she thought it was, this was going to be an opportunity of a lifetime for her.

'I want you to be in charge of the team that will work with the domestic violence cases.'

Yes! Ananya's hand clenched under the table in excitement, though she managed to maintain her poise.

'However, you have to first assure me of your complete dedication, Ananya. No more abandoning your duties at the drop of a hat. Think about it before you give me an answer,' Prachi advised.

'I don't need to.' Ananya leaned forward and let her excitement shine through. 'This is an opportunity that I've always dreamt of. I won't let you down. I promise.'

She didn't know how she would keep that promise, how she would keep Arvin from wrecking this for her, but she knew she would. She would figure out a way. She had to.

Looking at her determined expression, Prachi was convinced. She nodded and continued, 'The team that will report to you includes Ramya, Pankaj and Vaibhav. You will assign the caseload to each of them and ensure no mistakes are made. You will continue to work on your own cases, too, in addition to these duties. There will also be one fresher joining your team. Her name is Sania Aziz. She joins next week and can start off with research and other groundwork. You know the drill. After she completes a month or two, you can analyse her performance and then let her assist you on one of your cases. Let her get some courtroom experience.

'You and I will meet once in two days to review cases and any other pain points you might face. You will also be responsible for your team's revenue and billables. Keep in mind that the work you do also needs to bring in money. Remember to balance out the cases you want to take on for free with the ones that will keep this roof over our heads.'

'Right.'

One decisive tap of the pen on the table and Prachi stood up, forcing Ananya to her feet as well. 'That covers most of what I wanted to talk about. We'll discuss more in detail once I set things in motion.'

She was almost at the door when Ananya put out a hand to stop her. 'Thank you for the opportunity.'

'Don't thank me. You deserve it.' Prachi smiled. 'And I'm going to make you earn it.'

Ananya floated out of the office. Her head whirling with dreams, plans and a million other random thoughts, she got behind the wheel of her car.

Dropping her phone into the cup holder on the side, she was about to start the car when she noticed the missed call notification on her phone screen. It had been on silent the entire time she had been in the meeting with her boss. She scrolled through the call log. Sixteen missed calls from Arvin.

A chill ran down her spine. She could feel her elation, her pride and her excitement disappear like the air from a pricked balloon.

Slumping back against the car seat, she called him back.

'You called?' she asked the minute he picked up.

'We have to attend a dinner at the Marriott tonight. Be ready by nine.'

'I can't.' She wasn't sure where the words came from, but they were out there before she could stop them.

'Excuse me?' Frost coated his voice.

'I have work to complete before my appearance in court tomorrow. I was planning to work late.' Her pulse hammered in her throat, but she forced the words out, 'I'll be home, but working.'

'You can work after we come back,' he replied curtly.

'No, I—'

'Ananya,' he cut her off before she could utter another word. 'I don't have time for this. Be ready on time. Wear a saree. It's an engagement dinner.'

'Arvin—' She disconnected when she realized she was listening to the dial tone. She was a hypocrite. She had told Payal a little while earlier that no one had to live in a bad marriage, no one had to compromise.

But she knew that at nine that night, she would be ready for the engagement dinner, dressed in a saree.

Chapter 7

'What are you doing here?'

He'd earned the distrust in her eyes. Three days. It had been three very long days since he had started consciously avoiding Ananya. It hadn't taken long before he had realized that his utterly inappropriate attraction to his future sister-in-law was not dying a natural death or even an unnatural one.

Unfortunately, he couldn't avoid coming today. 'Arvin asked me to come.'

She stared at him for a moment before slumping in her seat. 'He's busy with work,' she said, her voice flat with resignation.

'He has a meeting.' Arnav took the seat across from her. The more distance between them, the better for his sanity.

'When does he not have a meeting?' she retorted.

Arnav shrugged. What could he say? This was Arvin's reality and it shouldn't really be coming as a surprise to her so close to the wedding.

'Miss Ananya Shastry.' The nurse at the door looked around the room questioningly.

'Isn't that you?' Arnav asked when Ananya made no move to answer. He turned to look at her only to find her frozen in her seat, her fingers holding on to the plastic chair in a death grip.

'Ananya?' Arnav moved to sit next to her. 'What's going on?'

'I can't,' she whispered. 'I can't do this.'

His heart jolted at the fear in her eyes as she looked at him. He took her hand in his and found it cold and clammy.

'What exactly is this?' he asked. 'What's happening right now?'

'I have...' she swallowed convulsively before continuing, 'I have to get my wisdom tooth extracted.'

'Do you have a phobia about being at a dentist's?' He gently chafed her hands between his. Beneath his thumb, her pulse raced erratically.

Ananya nodded, her lower lip trembling. 'That's why I wanted Arvin here.'

Something twisted in Arnav's belly, but he ignored it. Of course, she wanted Arvin here. She wanted her fiancé with her for support and not his brother like a cheap stand-in.

'Miss Ananya Shastry.' The nurse bellowed from the door, her voice getting more strident.

'Why don't we take this one step at a time?' Arnav asked, cupping her elbow with one hand and slowly getting her to her feet.

'We're here,' he told the nurse before she started yelling like a drill sergeant in an army boot camp again. With a curt nod, she spun on her heel and led the way towards the doctor's chambers. Arnav followed, Ananya clinging to his hand for dear life.

'Ah, there you are, Ananya.' The dentist was a cheerful middle-aged man who bore an uncanny resemblance to Santa Claus with his rather impressive white beard.

'And you must be the lucky man this young lady is getting married to.' He beamed at Arnav.

There it was again. The ugly slither of envy in his stomach. 'No, I'm just his unlucky brother,' he answered wryly.

'He's busy. Arvin, my fiancé, is busy.' Ananya burst into nervous chatter. *'He's always busy. He's a businessman, so…'*

'He's busy?' The doctor finished for her with a small smile. Ananya nodded, her face pale but set.

'Ananya, I promise you won't feel a thing after the injections.'

Arnav felt the tremor that ran through her at the doctor's words.

'Could we have a minute, Doc?' he asked.

The latter nodded and got busy setting out the injections that were needed for the procedure. Drawing her to a corner of the small room, Arnav tilted her chin up, so she couldn't avoid his eyes anymore.

'Hey, Anni,' he said softly. *'Are you in there?'*

For a minute, she didn't respond. Then a small smile touched her lips. 'Anni is curled up into a small ball and hiding.'

'You don't have to do this right now if you're not ready.'

'I'll never be ready,' she confessed. *'It took me a year to come this far.'*

'What can I do to help?'

Her eyes filled with tears at the simple question.

'No, no, no. No crying.' Going against every rational, sensible thought, he pulled her into his arms for a hug. Her arms went around him and held on tight, like it was the most natural thing in the world to do. Having her in his arms felt right. The feeling almost brought him to his knees. Gritting his teeth, he focussed on calming her down.

'Tell me what I can do to make you feel better and I'll do it. Whatever it is, I'll do it.'

'Can you hold my hand during the procedure?' she asked, her voice small.

'Of course,' he said, his cheek resting against her hair. *'I'm an excellent hand holder.'*

Ananya's shoulders shook as another suppressed sob ran through her. Arnav tightened his grip around her wishing he knew of a magic solution to rid her of her fears.

Behind them, the dentist cleared his throat. Their moment was over. The world was waiting.

Ananya sighed and looked up from where she'd buried her face in his sweater. Her gaze caught his. And for a millisecond, they let the world wait again. The moment was bittersweet, for it was over far too soon.

'Please don't let go.'

'I won't.'

'Promise?' she asked in a childlike plea for reassurance that broke his heart.

'I won't let go, Anni. I promise.'

∽

Ananya stared at the saree she'd chosen until spots danced in front of her eyes, the sequins on the turquoise net adding an extra shimmer. The perfectly draped saree was fancy and elegant.

She'd teamed it with diamond chandelier earrings and left her neck bare. Hair piled up in an artsy messy bun with tendrils framing her face, and legs slipped into silver stilettos finished her look. Her blouse was practically backless and held together with only a few strings, and her saree was tied below her navel, exposing a very sexy, toned waist. She knew Arvin would approve of her look.

One last spritz of perfume and she left the room. Gathering the pleats of her saree in one hand, she went down the stairs carefully to avoid tumbling down in a dramatic sweep. She turned at the landing and glanced down. The brothers turned as one to look at her. They were a sight to take any woman's breath away. Gorgeous, groomed and impeccably stylish in formal wear, they looked like every woman's dream come true. She wished she'd never set eyes on them.

Arnav sucked in a breath looking at her. The girl who'd smiled, laughed and bantered openly with him in the kitchen had disappeared. In her place stood the poised, sophisticated fashion plate. She looked beautiful and distant as if she'd left a part of herself behind, the part he loved. She had left his Anni behind.

Next to him, Arvin flicked a brief and dismissive glance at Ananya before turning for the door.

'We should leave or we'll be late' was all Arvin said.

Arnav stepped back and let Ananya precede him to the door. All the blood seemed to rush out of his brain and pool in the most inappropriate place at the sight of her backless blouse. There wasn't much there, just the expanse of smooth, silky skin. Rolling his tongue back into his mouth, he followed the two of them out to the car waiting for them.

He reached for the door to the rear seat only to have Ananya stop him.

'Please sit in the front seat.' Not waiting for a reply, she slid into the back seat and shut the car door in his face.

'*Haan, Bhai.* Come sit in the front.' Arvin called from the driver's seat leaving him with no option but to slide into the passenger seat in the front.

After two hours of bumper-to-bumper traffic, they still hadn't reached the venue. Two hours of deafening silence had left Arnav wondering if it was possible to freeze from cold vibes. He occupied himself by staring out of the window at the manic, frustrated crowd clogging the streets.

A taxi had hit a Mercedes ahead of it and the whole scene had erupted into a free-for-all in a matter of seconds.

'Fuck!' Arvin slammed his hands against the steering wheel, continuing to swear.

'Take it easy, bro. There's a cop coming over already. He'll clear up the mess soon enough.'

'Soon enough isn't going to get us to the damn party on time.' Arvin was grinding his teeth to powder now. 'Bloody shit!'

Arnav shrugged. This was Delhi traffic. What did his brother even expect? 'There isn't any point in getting worked up about it. It's not going to change anything. I don't understand—'

'No, you don't and you'll never fucking understand. I don't attend parties for the free booze. Big business deals are cracked at these things, but that's not something I expect you, with your tiny step-up from a fucking roadside dhaba, to understand.'

The silence that followed that outburst didn't thaw the chill in the car, it set it on fire. The atmosphere positively seethed with anger and hurt. No one spoke for what felt like forever until finally...

'The best food I've ever eaten was from a roadside dhaba.' The soft murmur from the back seat resounded in the explosive quiet. Arvin glared at the side mirror, pretending not to have heard her even though the tendons in his neck stood out like cords. Arnav turned to see Ananya staring out of her window at the fight that was dissipating. Cars were starting to rev their engines once again in anticipation of getting out of this mess.

She was defending him again. The past and present collided painfully. He had to take a deep breath to regain control. His eyes devoured the soft and delicate lines of her profile. The long eyelashes that framed her huge expressive eyes were resolutely trained on the scene outside. Her soft lips pressed into a tight line was the only indication of her tightly repressed anger.

Arvin slammed the car into gear and the car jerked forward when a miniscule gap opened up between the cars in front of them. Looking forward again, Arnav ignored his brother and his bad mood. The insult had slid through his armour and struck perfectly at the heart of his insecurities. Swallowing the hurt, he reminded himself that he was only there for a month, after which he could go back to his life. To his dhaba.

∽

They finally reached. Arnav honestly didn't know which one of the three of them was more relieved at the sight of the hotel. As soon as they entered the hall and paid their compliments to the newly engaged couple, he abandoned Arvin and Ananya and made a beeline for the bar.

'Scotch on the rocks.' He signaled the bartender, who nodded in acknowledgement.

A minute later, the drink was in his hand. He downed almost half of it in one gulp, letting the alcohol sear its way down his throat. It took nothing away from the hurt and anger that continued to burn in his gut. He should have been used to it by now. The insults, the condescension, even the snide jokes. Why did it still hurt? Why did he hope that his hard-won success would make them see him in a different light?

As he pondered his messy family relationships, he came to realize the exact reason behind why he was feeling the hurt today—it was because Ananya had been a witness to it all.

Call it pride, ego or just plain old self-respect, it still stung to know that she saw all of that. She'd witnessed it before, too, and even stood up for him in the past. Nothing had changed. But it was still true that being humiliated in her presence hurt more now than it had in the past.

In order to forget about the incident, he tried, unsuccessfully, to drown its memory with the rest of his Scotch. He was about to turn from the bar when a large hand came down on his shoulder.

'You're in Delhi and you didn't call me?' The boisterous accusation had him smiling even before he turned to face the massive turbaned man in front of him.

'Rajdeep!' Genuine affection warmed his voice as he hugged his childhood friend. 'I was going to call you.'

'Liar.' The accusation didn't carry much heat. 'It's okay. I understand.' And he did. Arnav could see it in his eyes.

At ease for the first time since the nasty scene in the car, Arnav refreshed his drink before moving with his friend to a nearby table. They were just settling down when a couple of Rajdeep's friends joined them. Conversation and alcohol flowed around the table. Even as he relaxed and participated in the ribbing surrounding him, his eyes searched for Ananya in the milling crowd.

He finally saw her standing amid a group of slightly older women, holding a glass of champagne in one hand. She looked effortlessly elegant. The saree skimmed her svelte figure and showcased it perfectly. The nonexistent blouse drew the attention of more than one man, not that she noticed any of it.

As he watched, Arvin strode up to the loosely huddled group. Sliding an arm around his wife's slender waist, he drew her closer.

Arnav frowned. Was it his imagination or did Ananya stiffen at the gesture? He was probably being overly sensitive to anything to do with her. As he watched, Arvin trailed a finger down Ananya's cheek and leaned in to whisper something in her ear.

As he fought the instinctive stab of pain that watching them together always brought him, he saw Ananya pull away. This time, he definitely hadn't imagined it. Her smile was strained. It was pathetic how easily he could read even the minutest change in her expression.

His gaze followed her slender body as she moved through the crowd and headed to the gardens visible through the bay windows. He wasn't the only one watching her. Arvin didn't follow his wife, but he watched her, with an inscrutable expression on his face.

Ananya disappeared from his view a few seconds later. Arnav saw his brother turn on his heel and head determinedly for the bar. Not wanting to get in the middle of a marital spat, he took another sip from his glass and stayed firmly in his seat.

'*The best food I've ever eaten was from a roadside dhaba.*'

The soft murmur rang in his ears. Damn. Shoving back from the table, he got to his feet and excused himself. She'd stood up for him when she didn't have to. The least he could do was check whether she was alright. He wondered whether this masochistic urge to be around Ananya would ever dissipate or if he was doomed to spend his life drawn to her like a moth to the flame.

She stood near the edge of the swimming pool, staring into the depths of the water as if it held the mysteries of the universe. Something in her expression had the hair on his neck standing.

'Hey,' he said, coming to stand next to her.

She didn't start at the sound of his voice or turn around but continued to stare at the water with that same blank, eerie expression. He simply stood next to her in silence and waited.

Finally, she turned around. 'You shouldn't be here.'

When she didn't say anything else, he shrugged. 'I tend to do a lot of things I shouldn't.'

It was true. A case in point being their feelings for each other. Their love story had been passionate but very short-lived. They'd loved and lost in what felt like the blink of an eye. It was only the pain that lived on. Endlessly.

She moved as if to walk past him and he shifted to give her space. But she stopped and turned around. She now stood directly in front of him, with only a few inches of space between them. That's all there was between him and the only woman he had ever loved. Taking a deep breath, he took a step back from her. He could have either done that or pulled her closer. Luckily, sanity prevailed.

'What are you doing out here, Anni?' he gently asked.

'I needed some fresh air.' She seemed to find the top button of his collarless shirt fascinating.

'Are you feeling sick?'

She laughed. It was the saddest sound he'd ever heard.

'I am.' The sad laugh was there again. 'I am feeling sick.'

Arnav gripped her chin and tipped her head back, so he could see her eyes. 'Do you want me to take you home? I can call a cab.'

'Home?' At the mere thought of the word and what it meant, she sounded sadder than before. 'No. I don't want to go home.'

'Has Arvin been giving you a hard time?'

Something that looked a lot like fear deepened her eyes. 'Why would you ask something like that?'

'Because of what you said in the car. The dhaba remark. You contradicted him for the first time.'

Some of the tension left her stiff shoulders. 'No. No, he isn't.'

He waited to see if she would say anything more, but she didn't. After a moment of silence, he asked, 'What can I do to make you feel better, Anni?'

'Nothing. Nothing will make me feel better.'

'There is always something.' He brushed a stray lock of hair that was falling in her eyes. 'We just need to find out what that is.'

Ananya reached up and caught his hand in hers. For one second, she cradled it against her cheek. She had lied. Having Arnav touch her with such care and tenderness always made her feel better. Tilting her head back to see his face in the dim lighting around the pool area, she asked, 'Why do you let him talk to you like that?'

They could hear the noise of the party even as they stood in the shadows by the pool. The lights from beneath the water lent a greenish hue to their surroundings. Everything seemed surreal.

He almost didn't answer. How could he explain a lifetime of regret, bitterness and frustration to her? 'My father hates me.' He saw Ananya check her instinctive denial and shrugged. 'It's okay. I've learned to live with it. Unfortunately, Arvin has to live with it a lot more than I do. All my father's hopes, dreams, frustrations…they're all pinned on him and only him. I got to escape, but he's stuck.'

'I don't think that's true,' Ananya murmured. 'Arvin enjoys

his work and his place in your father's life. He chose it.'

'Yes. But it would have been a happier life had my father not expected him to shoulder the responsibilities of both his sons.'

'That's hardly your fault.'

'My head knows that, but this,' laying a hand across his chest, he added, 'feels otherwise. His stress, pressure, frustration…more than half of them are because he's busy trying to carry out his responsibilities as well as mine. If he wants to snap at me once in a while,' he shrugged, 'I can live with it. After all, by the end of the month, at least I get to leave. He doesn't.'

Shoving his hands into his pockets, he stared over her head at the water that lapped the tiled walls of the pool.

'That's just one of the many ways I've wronged him. What I've done…' His words trailed into silence.

'He doesn't know,' she whispered into the quiet that surrounded them.

'Most days I pray he never finds out.'

'And the other days?' The soft question had his hands clenching in his pockets.

'The other days I want to tell him everything.' He kept his eyes on the minute ripples in the water. 'I want to tell him that I love a woman with every beat of my heart, with every breath in my body, with the very essence of my soul.'

He looked down at her. Dropping his shield, he let her see what she meant to him. 'I want to tell him that the woman who stands by his side is the very reason for my existence.'

'Don't.' It was the barest whisper.

'Not tell him or not tell you?'

'Don't love me.'

His voice trembled at her words. 'I wake up every day and remind myself that I have no right to love you like I do. Every. Single. Day. I hate myself. What kind of man loves his brother's wife? I hate myself, but I love you, Anni. I always have and God help me, I always will.'

Tears sheened her eyes as she looked at him. She tried to force words past the constriction in her throat.

He was the only one who had ever loved her. Ananya didn't know what to do with the maelstrom of feelings swirling inside her. She had walked away from the soul-searing emotions she felt for Arnav because guilt and duty had eaten her up from the inside.

The love she felt for him hadn't lessened over the years. If anything, it had grown impossibly stronger. But she was no longer the woman Arnav had fallen in love with. She was someone else, someone she didn't like much. And if she couldn't stand herself now, how could she let him love her?

'Ananya.' The hopelessly romantic moment shattered like cheap glass at the sound of Arvin's voice. She turned and saw him beckoning her over from the brightly lit verandah.

'Don't love me,' she whispered again. 'I don't want you to love me.'

His voice, too, dropped to a whisper. 'I would do anything within my power to grant you whatever you ask for, Anni. But this…this is beyond me. I can never stop loving you.'

Chapter 8

She was standing on top of the bar in a halter top and a skirt, which could have truly qualified as a scarf. Beside Arnav, Arvin stiffened. Even as they watched, she brought the microphone to her lips and started singing.

For a moment, Arnav couldn't believe his ears and then he started to laugh. She sounded like a frog with a sore throat. Around him, the rest of the pub had gone silent. He believed that was what one called an appalled silence. Although in his brother's case, it was more mortified than appalled.

'What the hell is she singing?'

Arnav couldn't stop laughing. He wasn't sure which song that was either. Ananya was mangling the song so badly, he didn't have a clue what it was supposed to be.

It had been Arvin's idea to crash Ananya's bachelorette party. Arvin's bachelor party, happening on the same night, had been a total bust. Arvin had insisted on a quiet, peaceful evening with friends. The poker game they'd organized had been quiet and peaceful enough to put them all to sleep.

Finally, Arvin had tossed his cards in the centre of the table and said, 'Fuck it! Let's go see what the girls are doing.'

And so, they'd come to see what the girls were up to. Arnav wiped tears of laughter while Ananya wound down with one last deafening screech. She was incredible.

'She's an embarrassment,' Arvin muttered. 'What the hell is she thinking? There are people here who know me.'

Arnav sobered at his brother's tone. It was frightening how easily his brother's behaviour mimicked that of their father.

'She's having fun,' he pointed out. 'It's not about you. It's about her.'

Flushed and laughing, Ananya tossed her hair back and handed the microphone down to the bartender standing behind her. Arvin turned on his heel and stalked out of the bar before she could even register his presence.

Arnav watched the door swing shut behind his brother's back. The rest of their friends stood around in an awkward circle looking anywhere but at each other. Ananya still hadn't noticed their presence. She was still up on the bar, her legs slightly apart, hands on her hips, hair a tangled but gorgeous mess around her smiling face. The bartender she was chatting with looked halfway in love with her. Arnav didn't blame him. There was also the possibility that the ass was taking the opportunity to look up her skirt.

Sighing, Arnav walked over to the counter.

'Ananya.' She didn't hear him over the music. Looking over her shoulder at the bartender, she hadn't yet noticed him standing near her feet.

He called her name again, only to get the same result. The noise in the bar was deafening and she wasn't looking his way. Arnav reached over and wrapped a hand around her ankle.

Startled, Ananya turned and looked down. Their gazes clashed and held. Arnav's hand tightened around her ankle. For the briefest moment, he let himself forget who she was and who he was.

'I won't let go, Anni. I promise.' His words came back to haunt him as he drank his fill of her. And then a wave of sound burst around them as their friends found each other.

Wordlessly, he released her ankle and held out a hand. She put her palm in his and let him help her off the counter. Her long and silky hair slid across his face as he lowered her to the ground. For a deliciously infinitesimal moment, her body rested against his.

And then it was over. Far too soon.

'Arvin went that way.' He gestured with his head even as he stepped back. 'You should go after him.'

'Why?' Ananya frowned.

'He's upset.' Arnav jammed his hands into his pockets. 'I don't think he liked seeing you up there.'

Temper flared in her expressive eyes. 'Then he shouldn't have crashed my bachelorette party. If he hadn't, he wouldn't have seen it.'

Arnav admired her spunk, but he knew his brother and his family. 'Don't you want peace?' he asked.

She smiled. 'Not at the cost of my right to live my life.'

'He'll sulk,' he warned her.

She shrugged. 'I won't pander to it. He'll have to figure it out for himself.'

And that was that. Respect and admiration formed a potent cocktail inside of him. With one last look at the door his brother had stormed through, Arnav sat down beside Ananya.

'You're a horrible singer,' he said affably.

'I know.' Ananya grinned. 'Doesn't change the fact that I love to sing.'

'Do you always do what you want?'

'Yes, as long as I'm not harming anyone. I make my own

happiness,' she answered, not even taking the time to think about it.

'And what happens if it is at the cost of another's happiness?'

Ananya paused, her glass halfway to her mouth. 'Then I'll just have to find a solution that is right for everyone involved.'

'Is life that simple?'

Ananya drained her glass. 'Life is always simple. We are the ones who complicate it.'

∽

Hands on his hips, Arnav stood inside his new café. It wasn't much—2,500 square feet, kitchen included. Small, cozy, perfect. Most importantly, it was his, unlike anything before, unlike the woman he loved.

Cursing himself for the thought that had popped up in his head, he ruthlessly brushed it aside and turned to look at his gleaming new kitchen. He walked forward, laid his knives down on the counter and looked around the place. He was interviewing candidates today and wanted them to see the work he had put into his kitchen.

He turned on the music, smiling slightly as Adele started to sing 'Rolling in the Deep', one of his favourites. He pulled out a knife and started to chop. He had had a recipe playing in the back of his head for the longest time. He had half an hour before the first candidate turned up and he was going to use it to sate his soul. Humming to himself, he got to work.

'God, that smells incredible.'

Arnav looked up from where he was stirring the sauce bubbling away on the stove. The speaker had long, curly hair tied back in a tight ponytail. She was on the shorter side, and dressed in black trousers and a black shirt. He could also spot her black nailpaint. *Very Goth!*

Glancing up at the clock, he realized more than half an hour had passed since he had started cooking. He was now looking at his prospective hostess.

'You're late,' he said mildly, turning off the stove and wiping his hands on his apron. 'I'm assuming you're Smitha?'

'The traffic was terrible,' she shrugged. 'And yes, I am.'

She came closer to the stove and took a whiff of the sauce. 'Do the staff at your restaurant get food, too?'

Amused, Arnav nodded. 'Yes, it is a perk, but we're not a restaurant, we're a café.'

She shrugged again. It seemed to be her default response to almost everything. Gesturing her over to a table just outside the kitchen door, he waited for her to take a seat. Ten minutes into the interview and Arnav knew he wasn't going to hire her. She had no interest in the food industry or customer service and was more bothered about whether she could parcel food home for her boyfriend.

After she left, he stayed in his seat for a moment making notations in her resume. He thought there might come a time when he would want to take another look at that.

He was just pushing back from the table when the door opened again. He saw a guy built like a tank filling the doorway.

'Yes?'

'Rajan Mishra. I'm here for the interview for a sous-chef.' His voice rumbled out of him sounding like a bag of rocks rubbing against each other.

'Great.' Taking in his rather intimidating size again, Arnav stepped back and pointed to the kitchen door. 'Shall we?'

Without a word, Rajan lumbered past him and through

the door. There was no other description for the way he moved. The man really did lumber.

Shaking his head in bemusement, Arnav followed. 'Where have you worked before?'

He found a sheet of paper shoved in his face in response. *A man of few words.* Taking the resume, he scanned it quickly.

'You haven't worked for very long,' he commented.

'No.' Rajan gave him a challenging stare. 'But I can cook.'

'Okay.' More than willing to give him a chance, Arnav boosted himself on to the stool behind him and said, 'Cook me something.'

Fifteen minutes later, he knew he'd struck gold. Had the Goth Girl hung around, she wouldn't have just asked for the leftovers but also licked the dishes clean.

Even before he could finish interviewing Rajan, the front door opened again, ushering in another candidate for the job of the hostess.

Several exhilarating hours later, Arnav had an almost fully staffed café. All he needed now were two more waiters and the café was all set to open. He wanted to rub his hands with glee. He was about to turn off the lights in the kitchen when he heard the front door open again.

Arnav frowned. He wasn't expecting any more candidates. Stepping out into the dining area, he stopped short at the sight of his brother in the doorway.

'May I come in?' Arvin's eyes were guarded, his stance stiff.

Nodding, Arnav braced himself for another round of unpleasantness.

Arvin walked in, his eyes scanning every inch of the renovated space. Walking past Arnav, he went into the kitchen. Following Arvin, Arnav stopped a step behind and waited to see what snarky comment his brother would make.

After a careful look around, Arvin turned to face him. He took a deep breath and then stopped. Arnav waited for him to speak, but when he didn't, he moved towards the kitchen counter and filled a bowl with the pasta and sauce he'd cooked earlier. Pouring a glass of Pepsi, he slid both across the countertop to him.

Arvin stared at the food in front of him. Arnav served himself another plate and sat down across from his brother. Not waiting to see what Arvin would do, he scooped up some and started to eat.

'I'm sorry about what I said yesterday...' Though the words were gruff, the sentiment came through clearly enough.

Arnav waved the apology away even before his brother could finish. 'Forget about it.'

His own guilt sat like a lump of lead in his chest. All Arvin had done was snap at him in a fit of childish temper, but he on the other hand...

'This place looks great.' Arvin's voice snapped him out of the familiar whirlpool of guilt and pain. 'What do you plan to call it?'

'Coffee Date.'

'Corny,' Arvin said with a smirk.

'Yes.' He laughed. 'But at least people won't forget about it.'

His smile faded at the serious expression on his brother's face. 'What's wrong?'

'I envy you.'

'Me?' Arnav forced a laugh this time. 'What exactly do you envy? The loans, the sleepless nights?'

'The freedom.'

The quiet words stopped Arnav mid-sentence. 'Why don't you tell Dad you want to quit?'

'And then do what? This is the only career I'm trained for.'

'Forget training. What would you like to do?'

After a long pause, Arvin said, 'Fly.'

'A pilot,' Arnav murmured. How had he never known this?

'That's impossible now.' Arvin knocked his knuckles against his prosthetic. 'I'll never pass the physical test.'

There was no getting around that. His brother, his baby brother, was hurting in ways he couldn't even imagine and all he could do was lust after his wife.

'Fuck it!' Arnav said. 'Let's go get drunk.'

∽

Ananya was sitting cross-legged on the bed working on a legal brief she had to submit the next day when Arnav knocked on her open bedroom door.

'Can I help you?' Ananya asked, eyebrows shooting up at his unexpected appearance.

'Hobby flying,' he announced.

'I beg your pardon.' Ananya stared at him. Was the stress of opening the café causing him to crack up?

'Where's Arvin?' he asked, ignoring her interjection.

'In the bathroom.'

She watched, amazed, as he walked across and pounded on the bathroom door. 'Arvin!' he yelled, sounding completely psyched about something.

'What's going on?' Ananya stood up at the exact same time as Arvin opened the bathroom door, almost causing Arnav, who was leaning against it, to lose his balance.

'What the fuck is going on?' Arvin growled. 'It's eleven in the night and—'

'Hobby flying,' Arnav said again. He sounded as excited as a child on Christmas Eve.

Arvin simply stared.

'Would anyone like to tell me what's going on?' Arnav's enthusiasm was contagious and had Ananya smiling at the two brothers.

'It's none of your business.'

Arvin's brusque reply had the smile disappearing from her face. An uncomfortable silence settled between the three of them.

'Let's go up on the terrace. I want a smoke.' Arvin walked out, leaving Arnav and Ananya facing each other across the expanse of the bed.

'He's just tired. He didn't mean to snap like that.' Even as he said the words, they rang false.

'Of course, he did.' Suddenly tired, Ananya sat down on the bed again. She stared at the legal papers in front of her until the words started to blur. She could sense Arnav standing there and staring at her.

'He's waiting for you,' she said, when he didn't move.

The dismissal in her tone was unmistakable, but he hesitated to leave her behind. She looked vulnerable, lost and completely defeated in that moment. Wanting to comfort her but not knowing how, he made a hesitant move towards her.

'Go, Arnav.' Ananya shut her eyes and turned away from his outstretched hand. 'If he gets pissed off waiting for you, he'll blame me for that, too. Just go.'

So, he went. He found his brother standing near the railing that lined the entire terrace. Hands braced on the top rail, he stared out at the sea of buildings and skyscrapers that littered the area surrounding their home. Lights flickered in windows, silhouettes moved behind gauzy curtains, horns blared angrily as late-night commuters cursed the ever-present traffic.

'What the fuck is going on with the two of you?'

Arvin didn't turn at the snarled question. He just stared at the night vista like it was something he'd never seen before.

'I asked you a fucking question.' The words were said with a murderous fury that seemed to consume him. He grabbed Arvin by the shoulder and spun him around.

'What. The. Fuck. Is. Wrong?'

'I don't think that's any of your business,' Arvin answered, his tone calm and totally devoid of any of the volatile emotions coursing through Arnav.

'You can't treat her like that. She's your wife!'

'Exactly. She's my wife, not yours and I'll decide how I can or can't treat her.'

The words fell like hammer blows across his mind and conscience. Taking a deep breath, Arnav fought to control his rapidly dissolving composure. This was the reason why he preferred staying away from home. He didn't want anything to do with his family and their sick madness.

'She doesn't deserve this crap.'

'No?' Arvin raised an eyebrow. 'And how do you know that?'

Resisting the urge to plant his fist in Arvin's face, Arnav took a step back and away from the temptation.

'No one does.'

'It doesn't look like she agrees with you.' The sardonic comment had his hands fisting.

'Nobody wants to be treated badly.' He'd had enough of this shit. Arnav turned away in disgust and started towards the stairs.

'Why is she still with me then? There's nothing stopping her from leaving.' The words, spoken without any emotion whatsoever, had Arnav freezing in his tracks. 'She's a lawyer, an exceptional one after all.' It might have probably been the first time he had heard Arvin compliment Ananya. 'So, why does a woman who specializes in getting women out of unhappy marriages stay in one?' Arvin asked him.

A very valid point.

'You're accepting yours is an unhappy marriage then?' Arnav asked.

Arvin started to laugh. Unfortunately, there was no humour in it. It was the saddest thing Arnav had heard.

∽

'Why?' Ananya's gaze shifted from the documents lying in front of her to Arnav standing in the doorway. 'Why are you still in this marriage?'

'That's none—'

'Of my business, I know,' he finished her sentence. 'But I'm still asking.'

Arnav felt like it was her answer that held the key to all the questions that twisted him up from inside. He watched her as she slowly got to her feet and faced him. The blank, dispassionate look on her face was chilling.

'I thought the two of you were having a brotherly bonding session on the terrace.'

'He got a call from the hotel and left.'

'And you found your way back to my bedroom?' Ananya asked mockingly.

'You can be as detached, rude or nasty as you want to be, but I'm not leaving without an answer.'

'Yet, you left the last time,' she shot back.

'Oh no.' Arnav shook his head. 'I didn't leave. You shoved me out of your life.'

'Let's see if I can do it again then? Get out,' Ananya said, her voice sounding strangely even and calm. 'I have work to do and no time to waste on you.'

Striding over, Arnav gripped her chin between his fingers and tilted her face up, so she couldn't avoid meeting his eyes anymore.

'Why the hell is someone like you continuing to stay in an unhappy and abusive marriage?'

'You don't know me. You sure as hell don't know the person I am today.'

'I know you're better than this. I know you deserve better than this.'

'Deserve you, you mean?' Pain and fury had her lashing out. 'That's what this is all about. Your ego can't take the fact that I don't want you.'

'You don't, do you?' The whisper of menace in his voice had her nerves fraying. 'Don't play games with me, Anni. It won't take long for either of us to prove that claim wrong.'

Ananya looked away. 'Arvin has never raised a hand on me.'

'He doesn't have to. You just sit there like a whipped puppy and take everything he dishes out.'

'How dare you?'

'How dare I?' Arnav thought he might explode from

the fury sweeping through him. 'How dare you? How dare you let him treat you this way? How dare you let *anyone* treat you this way? You fight for women's rights every single fucking day. You go out there and tell women that they deserve better. You fight for their rights...then why the fuck don't you fight for yours?'

He was shouting, but he didn't care. Emotions, which had been long suppressed, bubbled up and spilled over in a volcanic rush. 'What I feel for you defies logic, it is beyond rational thought. I would give anything to be able to wake up next to you, to see you smile like you mean it, to hear your crazy, wild laugh again. I gave you my heart that night and you walked away.' He took a moment to try and regain some semblance of control but found he couldn't. 'You chose to marry Arvin and I made my peace with your decision. I thought you chose a lifetime with him because you loved him and wanted him.'

Arnav walked up to where Ananya stood in frozen silence. Crowding her until she backed up against the wall, he leaned forward and braced his hands on either side of her. 'But you didn't. You chose a lifetime of pain, humiliation and degradation over the love I offered you. Why, Anni? Was the money so damn important?' Ananya flinched. A corner of her heart she hadn't known still existed in hope now shrivelled up and died. 'Was it worth it? You made this bed, now lie in it...isn't that what they say?' Gripping her chin in his hands, he forced her to meet his gaze. Unspent tears shimmered in hers, but she faced him without blinking. 'When you lie in this sick bed of yours, do the expensive silk sheets make it worth it?' They stared at each other in the dim glow of the night light on her bedside table. There were many emotions that still lay unvoiced. 'I hate the fact that I love you,' he whispered finally. 'But I wish I hated you instead.'

Releasing his grip on her chin, he stepped away from her before turning and walking out of the room he had no right to be in. Had he looked back, he would have seen Ananya crumple to the ground in a boneless heap.

But he didn't.

Chapter 9

'I'd like to make a toast.' Akhilesh stood, his voice cutting through the chatter filling the crowded room. He waited until the room was completely silent, his eyes moving from one table to the next till even the most hardcore chatterboxes stopped talking.

'It gives me great pleasure to welcome Ananya into our family,' he started his speech. The pompous tone brought a small smile to Arnav's face. His father could never resist the limelight. This was bound to be a long speech.

'We would like to assure Mr Shastry that Ananya will not be a daughter-in-law but a daughter in our house,' he paused, expectantly, and people obliged by applauding.

Arnav tuned out. His gaze wandered across the crowd that had gathered to attend his brother's engagement party that night. Arvin and Ananya sat by his father's side with polite smiles nailed to their faces.

They made a handsome couple—a fact that caused him to feel the now ever-present twinge of something he refused to name. He didn't want to be in a relationship. He was occupied and busy with his business and his life. And he thought that this completely inappropriate attraction would just die a natural death once this damn wedding was over and he could then go back to Mumbai, return to his life, his real life, and forget about this circus he found himself in the centre of.

'Of course, as Arvin is my sole heir and she is the one and only daughter-in-law of the Saxena household, she will enjoy a prominent position in society.'

His father's words pulled him away from his tangled thoughts. There wasn't anything new in the sentiment his father voiced, but by bringing it up in public, he was making it official. He'd certainly screamed the words in private more than once.

Arnav raised his glass to his father in a silent, mocking acknowledgement of his words. He saw Arvin glance at him, looking vaguely apologetic. A murmur permeated the room at his father's words. He ignored the embarrassed and furtive looks in his direction and kept his gaze fixed on his father.

Satisfied with his little bombshell, Akhilesh started to wind down. Arnav stayed planted in his seat till the bitter end of the speech. Soon, it was time for the ring ceremony. He stood, along with the other guests, and watched as Arvin slid a respectably massive diamond on Ananya's finger. She, in turn, slipped a gold band over his ring finger. The applause was louder this time around. Was he the only one who found it strange that the couple wasn't smiling?

People broke up into smaller groups and started mingling, which gave Arnav the opportunity to leave the room without looking like he was running away. He stepped out of the claustrophobic confines of the hall into the terrace and took his first real breath of the day.

Why did he bother? Why did he come home and let them insult him time and again? Although, it was only his father who did the insulting, what came from Arvin was more of a benign neglect. His mother waffled between loving him and being *embarrassed by him. He supposed, in a way, it was his penance.*

Voices approaching from behind had him instinctively backing further into the shadows he was already swathed in.

'Why didn't you say anything?' The indignant voice was instantly familiar to Arnav, a fact that had his gut clenching.

'I don't like creating scenes,' Arvin answered, his repressive statement a hint that Ananya clearly didn't want to take.

'He's your brother!'

'Let it go, Ananya,' Arvin snapped in irritation.

'Yes, let it go, Ananya.' Arnav added his own silent plea from the shadows.

'Don't you want to stand up for what is right?' Ananya clearly didn't get the message, both verbal and non-verbal.

'No,' Arvin answered. 'What I want is to enjoy my engagement party in peace without being lectured by my bride-to-be.'

'How would you feel if you were the one your father was disinheriting?'

'Relieved,' he replied curtly.

'What?' Her confusion was palpable even to Arnav, who was standing quietly, hidden from their view.

Arvin sighed. 'Don't get involved in all of this. It isn't worth your energy or mine.'

'But—'

'Leave it alone, Ananya.' With that abrupt order, Arvin turned and left the terrace.

Ananya let out a little scream of frustration, turning away from the doors to face the expanse of the lawn that stretched out below them. Resting her hands on the railing, she stared into the night, taking very loud deep breaths.

'You're doing the beagle thing again,' Arnav commented, unable to stay silent any longer.

Ananya whirled around to stare at him. She looked like the doll on top of a wedding cake. Her saree was all lace and net, and the bikini top blouse left very little to the imagination. It was very decorously covered with a diamond necklace that would have quite possibly made a huge dent in the national debt. Hell, at the very least, it would have completely paid off his business loan.

'It's not polite to eavesdrop,' she said.

'I was here first.' He felt obliged to point out, with all the maturity of a three-year-old.

'It's not right. What happened is not right.'

'Actually, if you think about it rationally, it makes perfect sense.'

She didn't say anything, just watched him in silence.

'Arvin is the one working in the family business. He's the one fulfilling all of my father's dreams. He lives with him, works with him and is the perfect son in every sense of the term.'

'It doesn't change the fact that you're also their son. Rejecting your right to your inheritance is...' she trailed off unwilling to put it in words.

'Rejecting me?' He finished her sentence for her.

She tipped her head to the side and watched him. 'And you don't mind that?'

Arnav shook his head automatically and then stopped. 'Of course, I mind.'

He'd never said those words out aloud. Why did he feel the need to now? he wondered. Then he looked at her and he knew.

He had told her to mind her own business, to butt out. He had told her that he didn't need defending. But not only did she continue to fight for him, she was the only one who did so.

'I don't want the business or the money or the properties. I

don't want any of it. I've built my own and it means more than anything they could give me. But you're right. When it comes to the matter of acceptance and rejection, I do mind. I don't hold any grudges against Arvin for any of it.' He needed her to know that. *'He has sure as hell earned it. Anyone who has to put up with my father night and day has earned every single bit of entitlement.'*

'But it hurts,' she added.

'Yes, it does,' he confirmed. How could it not?

'Legally...' she began.

'Don't, An—Ananya,' he corrected himself. She could now exist as Anni only in his mind. *'Don't go there. You're marrying into the family and you don't want to start your marriage on such a note, going to war with them, and that too over me. Don't be a lawyer right now. Just be their daughter-in-law.'*

Her troubled eyes met his. *'My conscience won't let me leave it alone. It's not right!'*

Arnav sighed. *'There is a lot in this world that isn't right. Why don't you focus on the battles you might actually win? This one, I promise you, is a lost cause.'*

She didn't answer immediately.

'Why is it so important to you that you do the right thing?'

'It's what my entire moral code is based on,' she said. *'I told you the other night why I became a lawyer. I believe in doing right and in righting wrongs. My parents are so absorbed in their individual lives, they never had time for anything beyond that. My dad has been busy with his work and my mom, with her social life. They have been two individuals who pursued their own lives with no interference from each other or anyone else. That is what works for them.'*

And, he wondered, where did that leave her. Arnav watched that delicate profile tighten with resolve.

She turned to look him full in the face. 'I was twelve when I decided to be a lawyer but not the kind my father was. I swore to myself that I would always do my best to do the right thing and if for some reason, I ended up wronging someone, I would do everything within my power to right it. It's what I live by. It is in many ways the foundation of my life. It may sound like a child's vow or promise, but I grew up watching my parents ruin people and their lives with a casual indifference just because they could. They had money and power, and an utter contempt for anyone who didn't,' she paused for breath. 'Don't get me wrong. I love them. I love them because they are my parents, but I don't necessarily like them. And most importantly, I won't be them. I won't! I won't turn my back on someone who's been wronged. I will do everything in my power to right a wrong and I will consciously make an effort never to harm or hurt someone.'

Arnav watched her standing there, her passion and fire lighting up her face and making her, if possible, even more beautiful. And he knew he loved her. It probably was inappropriate, wrong and in complete violation of her moral code of conduct, but he loved her with every breath of his being and every beat of his heart. There was no going back for him. Not now. Not ever. He couldn't control how he felt about her, but he could control what he did about it.

He took a deep breath and stepped away from her. 'If you really want to do what is right in this situation, you'll let this go. This is the best possible outcome for our family. All you'll do is stir up a hornet's nest if you don't.' She didn't look convinced. 'I'm happy, Ananya,' he said gently. 'And so are they. Let us all continue living that way.'

'Are you?' She raised her hand as if to touch his cheek but

stopped herself. 'Are you really happy?'

Some questions were better left unanswered.

Arnav felt the back of his eyes burn as the memory of that night streamed through his head. He'd fallen in love with her for the same reason he resented her today. He was the sacrifice she'd made at the altar of her moral code. In that moment, just for that moment, he hated her.

∽

Ananya stared at the gracious but imposing façade of the Ariaa Hotel in Delhi. Married to the scion of the family that owned it, she had been there a grand total of five times, each being social events that had required her to mark her attendance. She had hated every second of it. She had been on display, a trophy for the world to gawk at and speculate about.

Taking a deep breath, she stepped into the foyer. She'd barely reached the bank of elevators before the night manager caught up with her.

'Welcome, Mrs Saxena.' The smile on his face didn't completely conceal the surprise in his eyes. 'May I help you?'

She wanted to say no, but knew she wouldn't be able to reach Arvin without someone helping her.

'Yes,' she said with her most charming smile. The manager was so dazzled by it that he never realized that the smile didn't reach her eyes. 'I'm looking for my husband. He's working late tonight.'

'Yes, Madam. Sir is using one of the executive suites.' Punching the button to summon the elevator, he continued, 'Since it's so late, he decided to work from there rather than the office suites.'

Ananya followed the manager towards the elevator. He leant across and pressed the button for the fifteenth floor. They stood in silence while the numbers for each floor lit up in quick succession. The elevator doors opened on her destination floor.

She followed him to the end of the corridor where they stopped outside Suite 1504. Her pulse raced and a thin film of sweat sheened her upper lip. Discreetly dabbing at it, she rubbed her hand over her racing heart in a vain bid to calm it down. Her legendary poise had completely deserted her.

The manager pretended not to notice her sudden show of nerves. He knocked once and stepped back. It took a moment, but then the door was opened.

He was a mess. Hair dishevelled, half his shirt still tucked in while the other half lay wrinkled and loose. He still looked damn good. He was a very good-looking man, and that was a fact she often failed to see in the ugliness of their marriage. Surprise flashed in his eyes at the sight of her before it disappeared into his usual expressionless mask.

'Thank you, Karan.' He nodded at the manager, dismissing him without another glance. Stepping back, he held the door open for Ananya to enter the room. The door shut with a firm click the minute she crossed the threshold.

'What is it?' he asked without preamble.

Ananya wanted to run. She wanted to turn and run away like the hounds of hell were nipping at her heels, which did not seem like a bad analogy...her husband, she felt, was capable of doing more damage than any hound of hell.

'Ananya.' His impatient voice snapped her out of her thoughts. 'What do you want?'

What did she want? Ananya wet her suddenly bone-dry

lips with the tip of her tongue.

'I want us to try again.' She blurted out the words in a garbled rush.

Arvin frowned. 'What? I didn't catch that.'

Ananya rubbed her palm in small circles against her thudding heart. It didn't help with the panic racing through her.

'I want us to try again,' she said huskily.

Arvin froze. Neither of them moved for what felt like forever. When it didn't look like he was going to say anything, she started to speak, 'I know our marriage hasn't been what either of us wants, but I really think—'

'You think?' A faint sneer graced his lips. 'You *think?*'

Ananya stopped talking, sensing the scorn in his voice. A wave of exhaustion crashed into her. What was she doing? Why was she even trying to salvage their relationship?

Arvin strode away from her. He sat down on the side of the bed and fumbled at the straps of his prosthetic. A grunt escaped him as he wrenched it off the stump. His trouser leg fell forward in an empty cascade over it. Tears clogged Ananya's throat as she stared at the prosthetic in his hand.

'I'm sorry,' she whispered. 'You have no idea how sorry I am.'

'No idea? No idea???' Arvin roared. 'You think I don't know? I live with the goddamn knowledge every single day of my miserable life. Every. Single. Fucking. Day. Do you think I want your pity? Your guilt? Your fucking shame?'

He heaved the prosthetic against the wall with a yell that resounded in the hotel room. It crashed into the mirror on the wall to Ananya's right. The glass splintered into a million fragments, and so did her heart.

She took a shaky step back from the furious man who

stood to face her. Sweat trickled down her forehead and into her eye. She blinked it away without taking her gaze from Arvin.

'What more can I do?' The words were torn from her throat. Years of anguish, hurt and misery spilled out. 'I've paid for it every way I can think of. I've given you my life, my self-respect, my loyalty… I've given you everything. What more do you want from me?'

'Do you love me?' The question was a verbal slap in the face that silenced her impassioned plea. Ananya opened her mouth to reply but found her voice had deserted her. 'Do you?' he repeated, watching her face carefully.

'No.'

The whisper had more impact than any of the heated words exchanged so far. His shoulders sagged as he turned from her to face the large bay windows that lined the far wall of the room. He leaned against the wall, taking its support to stay upright.

'Get out.' The words were quiet, not the intent.

'Arvin, please…' She couldn't leave with those being the last words. 'I want us to give our marriage another chance. I want us to try and have the marriage we once hoped for before—'

'Before you fell in love with another man?'

Ananya fell silent.

'No comeback to that?' he mocked her without turning around.

'I've been a good wife to you,' she said stiffly.

'A good wife?' he retorted with a laugh. Finally, he turned and faced her. 'Aren't you going to ask me if I love you?'

All she could do was stare at him, stare at the man

who was both her husband and a complete stranger. He had intimate knowledge of her body but none of her heart.

'I despise the sight of you.'

His words pierced her heart like nothing he'd said or done to her so far. She felt the last vestiges of her prior self die a slow, painful death. Without another word, she turned on her heel and left the room, shutting the door behind her.

In the quietness of the room, Arvin whispered, 'But I still love you.'

He'd finally said what he wanted to, but his words would stay unheard. Ananya was gone.

∽

'He lost his leg because of me.'

At the sound of Ananya's voice, Arnav shut his eyes. Fury and hurt had combined to drive him from the house to his café, where he was sitting, crouched near the kitchen cabinet, sorting and settling all the new equipment that had been delivered. He stayed where he was with his back to her. He didn't hear anything more as he continued to unpack cartons of kitchenware.

After a moment, she came to kneel beside him. Slender, pale fingers reached out to pick up a set of deboning knives. She picked up one and traced the outline of the blade with an unsettling focus.

'It was an accident, Anni.'

She didn't answer. She didn't even look at him, though she was right next to him. Her delicate profile was inches away from his traitorous fingers. Grabbing a large frying pan, he added it to the pile already lining the shelf in front of him.

'Tall, dark and handsome... Isn't that what every girl dreams of? Arvin was everything I dreamt of, and more.'

Arnav ignored the sharp stab of pain her admission caused and continued stocking pots and pans like his life depended on it. In a way, he supposed it did.

Seemingly oblivious to the damage she was wreaking on his barely beating heart, Ananya continued, 'I couldn't believe it when your parents approached mine with the proposal. I had had a crush on him forever. We'd been friends, good friends and hung out together in the same group, but I knew he didn't see me that way. He had always had a girl with him. A gorgeous, popular, successful girl, who wasn't someone boring like me. All I was to him was a great bud. And then, your parents came home.'

She put the knife down and straightened. Arnav stayed where he was on the floor. At her feet. Very apt. Very symbolic. He wanted to bang his head on the wall next to him.

'My parents were over the moon. They couldn't possibly have imagined a better marriage offer for their daughter than Arvin Saxena, heir to the Saxena empire. Handsome, educated, rich, successful. He was everything one could have asked for.'

His thoughts were now circling around the knife she'd been staring at. He wanted to grab it and stab himself with it. It would probably hurt less than her long-winded love saga.

'He overwhelmed me. From the first time we met until the moment I said yes...although me saying yes was considered a given by everyone. He was...' her voice trailed off for a moment and then she finished, '...magnificent.'

Arnav stared at the ladle in his hand. Magnificent. There wasn't much you could say to that. Very carefully, he sat the ladle down in its spot on the shelf in front of him.

'I was so excited about the wedding.' She trailed her fingers down the edge of the nearest kitchen counter as she slowly walked its length. 'The clothes, the functions, the jewellery, the visiting friends and family... It was all a frantic whirl of excitement. And then I met you.'

Arnav looked up at her. She still wasn't looking at him. She continued to watch her fingers as they gently skimmed the kitchen counter.

'Big, surly and arrogant with everyone around,' Ananya laughed.

Well, that certainly was a far cry from magnificent, Arnav reflected wryly.

'You irritated me on every possible level.'

Great. Arnav got to his feet. There was only so much his battered ego could take.

'I think—'

'I wanted to ignore you, but no matter how hard I tried I couldn't,' Ananya continued talking like he hadn't spoken. 'You were this pebble in my slipper that I just couldn't seem to remove.'

Arnav scrubbed the palms of his hands across his face. This just kept getting better. He didn't know where this conversation was going, but he needed it to end soon, preferably before it destroyed whatever little self-respect he was left with.

'He was everything I dreamt of and I was so ready to love him with all my heart,' and finally, she looked up and met his eyes, 'but I fell in love with you.' Arnav's heart stopped. 'You knew that. You knew how desperately I was in love with you.'

Was. The word echoed in his head. *Was.*

'You married him,' he finally said the words that burned through his gut every day. His fingers vised around the spatula he still held. 'You chose him.'

Ananya didn't answer for the longest time. Then she said, 'I called it off. I told Arvin when we were driving home from the sangeet that I was in love with someone else.' Arnav stopped breathing. 'I never told him who it was that I loved.'

'Why?' he asked hoarsely.

'I thought it would be too big a betrayal at the time. I wanted to break it to him slowly.' She smiled sadly. 'I knew Arvin wasn't in love with me at that point. I was just the suitable bride, the perfect foil to his image. We'd been friends before and became even better friends over our courtship period, but that's all it was at that point. A friendship. I thought that all I would be doing was denting his pride, but instead I took his leg.'

'Anni—' Arnav took a step forward but stopped when she stepped back.

Ananya held her hands up, palms out. 'Don't. Please don't touch me. I fell in love with you so hard and so fast, I didn't know what hit me. All I knew was that I didn't care about any of the things that previously consumed me. All I wanted was you. I didn't stop to think about the repercussions of what I was setting in motion. I couldn't see beyond the storm of emotion you caused in me. I couldn't see Arvin.'

Ananya stopped. How could she ever explain to someone what she barely understood herself.

'I'm the reason we had that accident. I'm the reason Arvin lost his leg. I'm the reason his entire world changed.'

'And to make up for that, you married him.'

'Yes. So, I married him,' she echoed his words. 'I wanted to make him smile again, make him happy again, make him Arvin again. I thought marrying him would heal him, but I destroyed him.' She raised her shattered eyes to his. Arnav desperately wanted to reach for her, to hold her and comfort her. But again, she took a step back from him. 'I destroyed him,' she repeated, 'and I destroyed us. I'm a horrible person.'

'No, Anni. You're not.' Arnav couldn't stand to see what she was doing to herself.

'I am.' Her breath caught on a sob. 'I am because…'

'Because?' Nothing she said would ever make him believe she was anything but the girl he loved.

'Because I never stopped loving you.'

The words stopped his heart.

'Years. I've spent five years trying to fix the mess I made, but how can I? How can I ever make my husband happy when all I see is you?'

She came closer as she spoke until she stood right in front of him. Tipping her head back, she looked up at him, all pretenses forgotten. 'I love you. I loved you then. I love you now.'

And then she kissed him.

Chapter 10

'You shouldn't be here.'

'I know.' Still she didn't move from the threshold of his room.

'Anni, if anyone saw you here, it would be a disaster.'

'Then invite me in.' The boldness of her words contrasted sharply with the tremor in her voice.

Arnav stepped back in wordless invitation. Whatever she had to say, it would be better to hear it in the privacy of his room. If she was discovered hovering outside his bedroom door at two in the morning—he shuddered to think what the outcome of that would be for her. He couldn't care less about himself. His future in this family was precarious even at the best of times.

'Did you need something?' He kept his tone carefully neutral. The tiny shorts and tank top she wore made it hard for him to maintain a neutral choice of words.

Ananya wrapped her arms around her midriff in a frightened gesture that had him aching to hold her. Instead, he jammed his hands in the pockets of his jeans to keep them from following through on the intent. He soon realized he was wearing nothing but his jeans.

'Anni?' he prompted when she didn't say anything. 'Did you need something?'

'Yes. You.'

The word resounded in the deafening silence that followed.

'Don't.' Raw and unforgiving, his hoarse reply stalled her forward motion towards him. 'Don't.'

'I can't do this anymore,' she whispered. 'I can't lie to myself about how I feel.'

Arnav turned from her to stare blindly at the wall. He didn't want to hear this. Knowing he loved the woman who was marrying his brother was hard enough, but knowing she loved him back was sheer torture because nothing could come of this. Whatever their differences, he loved his family and he would never do this to them.

Ananya's hands came around him from behind. Crossing them over his bare chest, she hugged him tight. A hard shudder racked his body as the soft, silken heat of her skin surrounded him.

'Don't turn away from me, please,' she begged. 'Nobody will understand and if you don't either—'

His hand came up to cover the one she had resting over his heart, a traitorous heart that pounded wildly under her palm.

'He's my brother. I can't do this.' Conviction strengthening his voice, he said, 'I won't do this.'

'Do you love me?' Her heart in her eyes, she moved to face him. 'Tell me you don't and I'll go away.'

A thin sheen of sweat broke out on his forehead. 'Anni, please.'

'Please what?' Her eyes dared him to admit the truth that shone in her own. When he didn't answer, she gathered her shaky courage and reached up. Cupping his stubbled cheeks, she brought her lips to his.

Arnav froze. Her lips moved hesitantly over his, searching for a response but finding none. It took every ounce of will power to keep himself from claiming her the way he wanted to.

Humiliation seared through her as he stayed as still as a statue. Stepping back, she shut her eyes to keep mortified tears from spilling over.

And that is when Arnav lost the battle. A startled gasp escaped her before he claimed her mouth in a kiss that drove every rational thought from his brain. His fingers clenched in her tumbled hair, pulling her head back and deepening the kiss.

A low moan escaped her as she slid her fingers through his hair and held onto him like her life depended on it. And it did, in more ways than one.

∽

They came together in a fury of need and emotion that threatened to consume them both before they were done. Reason, morals, common sense, all went flying out of the window as years of pent-up longing and desire erupted between them.

Arnav buried his hands in her hair, tugging her head back. An incoherent moan escaped her as she allowed him to deepen the kiss she'd initiated. It had been so long since she'd been touched with tenderness, with care.

Arnav's hands were careful with her body, his fingers gentle against her skin. She felt the ice that had encased her for so long crack and splinter in a glorious rush of sensation. Greedy now to feel more of him, she slipped impatient fingers under his soft cotton T-shirt. Taut skin across lean muscles burned against her hand. Spreading her palms out against his back, she urged him closer against her, wanting his warmth and his passion to heat her from the inside out.

In response, Arnav picked her up and backed her against

the wall. Ananya wrapped her legs around his waist and let him take over. She could feel the hard length of his erection intimately pressed against her. In response, she gripped him tighter with her thighs.

A ripping sound filled the air and her shirt fell to the floor. Arnav's eyes were hot as they took in the cream-coloured lace that covered her breasts.

He bent his head, his breath coming in short, hard bursts against her skin. Shivering a little, Ananya curved a hand against the back of his head and held on. When his lips found her nipple through the lace, she whimpered.

The sound shot straight through Arnav's self-control. Abandoning all attempts to go slow, he yanked her bra out of the way and took her into his mouth. Ananya moaned, driving him further over the edge. With his other hand, he tugged at her trousers. He let her unwrap herself from around his waist long enough to shed her trousers and panties.

Ananya barely managed to kick them out of the way before he hauled her up against him and brought her mouth to his again. She pulled at his T-shirt with impatient hands managing to get it over his head and to the side with just a minute break in the kiss that was singeing her brain.

Arnav's arms went around her, drawing her close. A soft sigh escaped her and feathered across his lips as her breasts pressed up in an intimate embrace against the damp heat of his chest.

Drawing back an inch, Arnav murmured, 'Anni, my Anni.'

The sorest parts of her battered heart healed a little at the way he looked at her, like she was precious, like she mattered.

Tears shimmered in her eyes making him shake his head. 'No crying. We're done with that. Whatever happens after this, we face it together.'

Years of neglect and abuse had her asking for reassurance. 'You won't change your mind?'

Arnav was already shaking his head even before she finished voicing the question.

'I never did,' he reminded her. 'You're my forever, Anni.'

'You're mine.' With that, she leaned in and brushed her lips with his again. 'No more talking.'

In response, Arnav leaned down to kiss the slender curve of her neck. Ananya's head fell back in surrender. He stepped out of his jeans before letting her naked body rest against his own. At the contact, everything inside of him shuddered, sighed and finally settled into place. His world righted itself.

Ananya's cool hands came to rest on his buttocks, stroking and massaging. She murmured a protest as he shifted away from her. Letting his hands rest on the curve of her hips, he started to kiss his way down her body. His mouth paid homage to one breast even as his hand did the same to the other. Tremors racked her body even as he dropped to his knees to place a light kiss against her navel. Her stomach quivered.

'Arnav.' His name sounded like more of a plea than a protest.

Letting his fingertips rest against her lips to silence her, he blew lightly against the sensitive skin below her navel. When her knees started to buckle, he placed both hands on the curves of her hip and anchored her. Drawing her legs slightly apart, he looked up at her from where he knelt before her.

Her eyes hot and hooded, body bare and open to his gaze, she stared directly at him, letting him see her. Every single part of her.

Arnav dropped every last barrier and let her see exactly what she meant to him. Her breath caught and hitched at the emotion that swarmed in his gaze. Her tremulous fingers gently stroked back the lock of hair that was falling into his eyes.

'I love you, Anni.'

With that simple declaration, he leaned forward and kissed her. His mouth and tongue, like hot silk, against the most intimate part of her. Ananya fisted her hands in his hair and held on, so she didn't collapse in a quivering heap at his feet. Fireworks sparked in her system as sensation bombarded her. Moaning, she unconsciously urged him closer with her grip on his hair.

Accepting the invitation, Arnav let himself worship her. With each stroke, each caress, Ananya felt her body tighten into an unbearable coil. Giving herself over to the sensation, she felt her spine arch as with one last flick of his tongue she came undone.

Arnav gathered her into his arms as she slid onto the floor in a boneless heap. She turned in his arms and pulled his head down for another kiss. Still joined at the lips, she leaned back until she was flat on the ground, with his lean, hard length pressed against her. She felt incredible, satiated and yet ready for more.

She spread her legs, so he was cradled intimately against her. Tightening her grip on his buttocks, she dug her nails into his skin in silent urging.

Arnav raised himself on his forearms and looked down at her, this woman who held his heart in the palm of her hand.

'You're sure?' he asked quietly.

'Yes.' Locking one leg around his waist, she urged him

forward. With a groan torn from the depths of his being, Arnav slid into the warm, welcoming heat of her body. Silken skin stretched and gripped him in an intimate embrace that almost had him losing what little control he had left.

Dropping his head to her shoulder, he started to move. Ananya's fingers stroked the hair at the nape of his neck causing him to shudder in response. Slowly, he started to pick up the pace until he was pounding into her. Ananya wrapped her legs around him and took him on the ride of his life.

Harsh, guttural gasps escaped him as he felt his body start to tighten. Turning his face to the side, he took her lips in a kiss that was both a promise and a penance. His release tore through him like a freight train and took with it his last coherent thought.

∽

Later, much later, still in his café, Arnav raised himself on one arm and looked down at her. She looked like a cat who'd been caught lapping up an entire bowl of cream and couldn't care less.

'No regrets?' he asked with a smile.

And just like that the peace of the moment was shattered. Shadows clouded her eyes as she sat up. She reached for her shirt only to remember it was torn and wouldn't cover anything. She didn't meet his eyes as she picked up his T-shirt instead and shrugged into it. The hem brushed her knees as she sat cross-legged across from where he still reclined.

'Some regrets,' she said as she finally looked at him.

Hurt lanced through him at her answer. Suddenly conscious of his nakedness, he sat up and pulled on his jeans. Zipping up, he felt like he was donning armour, but he knew there was no point. This battle was going to leave him bloody by the end of it.

'I'm sorry you feel that way,' he said stiffly. He turned to look at her. She looked like a lost waif in his T-shirt that hung in voluminous folds around her with tangled hair brushing her waist and tightly clenched fingers in her lap. 'I'm sorry we didn't use protection. I wasn't prepared for what happened today.'

Ananya shook her head at that. 'That's one regret you don't need to have. I'm on the pill.'

'I don't regret anything. I could never regret you, Anni. I differ from you there.'

Distress and then sudden understanding dawned upon her. 'No. No. You got me wrong. I don't regret you.' Jumping to her feet, she inched closer to him. Her slender fingers reached up to cup his cheek and keep him anchored to her and to the moment.

'I don't regret this. Not for a single moment,' Ananya whispered.

Agitation had her fingers trembling against his face. Wordlessly, Arnav reached up to cover her hand with his. The calm strength of his fingers stilled the nervous tremor in hers.

'What then?' he asked.

The time for games was over. Now it was time to make their choice and stand by it.

'I regret hurting Arvin. I regret what this will do to your family and, most of all, I regret what it will do to your relationship with your family.'

It would entirely end his relationship with his family, and

he knew it. Arnav accepted the fact. The day he would hold Anni's hand in public would be the last day he would see any member of his family. There would be no forgiveness for this and he wanted none. Anni was not his mistake that needed to be forgiven. She was his and that was all that mattered.

He had tried to forget her, to move on. God was his witness. He had tried, but all his attempts had been as futile as trying to forget to breathe. Anni was not just his choice, she was his hope. She was his dream and, in every way, his prayer.

'They'll never forgive us, Arnav…' she whispered, '…and Arvin…this will be the last straw for him.'

A pang pierced through Arnav's heart at the thought. He could never regret Anni, but he wished it didn't come at the cost of his brother's pain. But he knew that his brother didn't want her. Arvin had had five years with Anni, to love her, to cherish her, to build a life with her. And he'd done none of that. Instead, he'd demeaned her, abused her and, on some level, even broken her. For that, Arnav would never forgive him.

'We did the right thing for everyone before,' Arnav said, choosing his words carefully. 'It didn't work out well for anyone. Not them. Not us. Maybe it's time to do the right thing for us now.'

'How can something so wrong feel so right?' The anguished question had him holding her close.

'Love is never wrong, Anni. The circumstances are wrong, but what we feel is not wrong,' he said fiercely.

Ananya broke down. Harsh, shuddering sobs racked her body as she held onto Arnav. She lanced the festering ulcers of pain, regret and guilt and let it all pour out in an avalanche of emotions. She cried for the girl she'd been, for the girl she was now, and for the two men she'd loved and hurt.

She cried for the families she was going to destroy, for the life she was leaving behind and the one she so desperately wanted to begin.

∽

The first rays of the morning sunlight filtered through her bedroom curtains when Ananya walked into it. Arvin was sitting on the recliner by the bed with his laptop open. A half empty glass of whisky sat on the table beside him. That didn't bode well for her or the day ahead, especially considering what she was planning to tell him.

Walking past him without a word, Ananya went into the bathroom. She flicked the switch on for the heater and walked over to the sink to splash some water on her flushed face. Her eyes were red and puffy. Everything inside her had shifted in momentous ways.

The heater clicked behind her signalling her water was ready. Shedding her clothes, Ananya stepped into the shower. She sighed as the practically boiling water cascaded down her bare skin. Steam rose and fogged the cubicle around her making her feel like she was in a private cocoon. Ananya let herself enjoy the illusion. Sometimes, illusions are all you have. Reality awaited her on the other side of the door. So, for these few moments, she basked in the privacy of her steamy cocoon.

It didn't take long for the illusion to shatter. Someone slid open the bathroom door. Ananya froze. She knew that noise and what was worse was that she knew what it meant.

Ananya turned off the shower and reached for the towel hanging on the rack behind her. Wrapping it around herself as firmly as possible, she stepped out of the cubicle and faced Arvin.

He leaned against the basin counter and stared at her with absolutely no expression on his face. As she stepped out of the shower, he stepped towards her. Coming closer, he laid a hand on the curve of her neck holding her in place in a consciously dominating position.

Ananya gasped, panic thrumming through her veins. Before she could speak, he tugged at her towel with one hand. The fabric came apart without any struggle. She stood before him, naked. Unwilling to let him see the shame coursing through her body, Ananya held his gaze unflinchingly.

'Arvin—'

He said roughly, 'No more talking.' He caught her elbow with one hand and spun her around, her naked back pressed up against the soft fabric of his T-shirt. His good leg shifted between her thighs spreading them. She could feel him hard and ready against her.

Pulse pounding in a furious mixture of fear and shame, Ananya swallowed hard and said, 'No.'

The arm reaching around her waist froze near her navel. 'No?' he queried softly.

'No,' she repeated.

After another dangerously quiet moment, Arvin spun her around and stared at her. His breath smelled strongly of the whisky he'd consumed. Ananya's already queasy stomach lurched unpleasantly. Naked and vulnerable, she faced him, determined to stand her ground.

'No. Not anymore.'

For a long unfathomable moment, Arvin stared at her unblinkingly. Then, he nodded once before walking away.

The bathroom door shut behind him.

Shaking from the aftermath of what had just transpired, Ananya slid down to the floor. She hugged herself in a futile attempt to control the tremors that racked her body. Her fingers were still trembling when she groped for the towel he had pulled off her. She wrapped herself in it again. It took her three tries before she could knot it around herself firmly. Clutching her towel like it was armour, she pushed herself to her feet.

Now was as good a time as any to finish this. She would ask Arvin for a divorce and then… Her mind trailed off, unable to grasp the future she was attempting to reach for. Well, then she would see what came next. One step at a time.

She grabbed the first pair of shorts and T-shirt she could find in her cupboard and struggled to put them on. Her hands and legs still shook.

Her wet locks of hair dampened her T-shirt. Ignoring the spreading wet patch across the fabric, Ananya pushed the bathroom door open.

'Arvin, I need to talk to you,' she announced as firmly as she could. But it was too late. The room was empty and she was talking to herself.

Chapter 11

'Didi, kaun sa akshar likhu? *(Madam, which letter should I put in?)*'

Ananya started out of her daze at the mehendiwali's question. 'Kya?'

'Aapke haath mein? *(In your hand?)*' She gestured towards the intricate henna designs on Ananya's hands.

'A,' Ananya said through numb lips. 'A.'

'Poora naam likhu ya sirf A? *(Should I write the entire name or just A)?*

'Sirf A *(Just A),*' she whispered as she watched Arnav lower his head to listen to something his mother was saying. Her heart seemed to squeeze inside her until she fought to take her next breath. *Oh God! What was she going to do? She loved him. She was getting married in three days and she was in love with her fiancé's brother.* Panic erupted inside her and she yanked her hand out of the mehendiwali's hand, smearing the mehendi on her palm.

'*Didi!*' The distress in the woman's voice barely penetrated as Ananya shot to her feet. Her dupatta slipped on to the floor as she ran through the crowd and into one of the rooms that bordered the hall they'd rented for the function. Slamming the *door behind her, she rested her back against it and tried to steady her breath. It wasn't working. Her vision started to blur and black dots danced in front of her eyes.*

Someone knocked on the door behind her startling her out of the crouch she'd slid into. Ananya struggled to her feet and stepped away from the door even as the knocking intensified.

'Ananya.'

Her heart jumped at the sound of his voice. She swiped her hand across the sweat beading her upper lip.

'Ananya, are you okay?' Arnav kept his voice low, but it came through the door loud and clear.

Ananya shook her head, her mind too scrambled to realize he couldn't see the gesture.

'Ananya.' His volume went up a little. 'Open the door.'

'No.' It was slightly louder than a whisper, but she knew he'd heard her because of his sudden silence.

'Are you okay?' he asked again after a pause, his voice so tender it brought tears to her eyes.

'No. I'm not,' she said, her voice more than a little hysterical as she blurted out, 'I'm in love with you. How can I be okay?'

All Ananya heard for a few seconds was the thunderous roar of her heart. And then finally, 'Anni, please open the door.'

'No.' For some reason, it was crucial for her to make sure she did not open the door. She'd had more courage the previous night when she'd gone to his room. But now that she knew what it felt like to be with him, to hold him, to share a heartbeat of intimacy with him... A choked sob escaped her. 'I can't do it. I can't marry Arvin.'

'Anni,' he said her name in a whisper.

'I can't.' She, on the other hand, was getting dangerously louder. Consciously struggling to calm down, she said, 'I'll tell

him. He'll be upset at first, but even he won't want to be married to someone who doesn't love him.'

'And then what, Anni? What happens then?'

'I don't know,' she whispered. 'But at least I won't be ruining his life by marrying him when I love you.' It was idealistic. It was stupid. It was wrong. But Ananya was going to do it. 'Do you love me?' she asked with a pounding heart.

Hearing nothing in reply, Ananya slumped against the wall behind her.

'He's my brother,' he said finally.

'That's not what I asked you.'

'Open the door, Anni,' he said roughly. 'I don't want to have this conversation through a fucking door.'

'No.' Ananya shook her head. 'First, answer me.'

'I can't love you. I have no business loving you...'

'But?' She prayed to God there was a but...

'But I do.'

As soon as she heard his simple declaration, she opened the door.

∽

Ananya walked in from a long, painful day at work to find her mother-in-law waiting for her in the living room.

'Ananya beta, where have you been?'

Ananya looked down at herself. She was in a simple cotton salwar kameez and her black lawyer's coat with about ten messy files jammed under one arm and her laptop bag slung over the other. There was only one place she could have been.

Ananya sighed. She was in a foul mood and it wasn't her

mother-in-law's fault. Biting back the sarcasm that rose to her lips, she answered, 'At work, Ma. Was there something you wanted?'

'Not anymore. I was trying your number all day.'

Ananya fumbled in her pocket for her phone and pulled it out. There were fifteen missed calls.

'I'm sorry. I was in court and the phone was on silent. Was it something important?'

'Well,' Shayla said with a frown, 'at that time it was. Arvin wanted to pack his white shirt. The one with the blue-and-white-checks piping? We couldn't find it anywhere.'

'Pack?' Ananya repeated cautiously.

'Yes. He left for Chennai on work. Didn't he tell you?'

Ananya wondered how to answer that without worrying her mother-in-law. 'He might have mentioned it. I've been a bit occupied with my latest case. It must have slipped my mind.'

'You modern couples and your modern marriages,' Shayla grumbled. 'If I hadn't been there to pack for my husband and wave him goodbye on his business trips, my marriage would have been as good as over.' Her own marriage was as good as over. The thought slammed through Ananya's fragile veneer of normalcy and shattered it to pieces. Biting her lip hard enough to taste blood, she stayed silent.

'Anyway, you're home now.' She laid a soft hand against Ananya's cheek. 'Have something to eat and get some rest. You look tired.'

The gentle touch and simple compassion had tears springing to Ananya's eyes. Her already over-burdened conscience sagged a bit more. Here was a woman who had been more of a mother to her than her own and she was betraying her. She blinked back the tears before they could spill over and worry Shayla.

'Ma—' she began only to be cut off by Arnav's gruff voice.

'I'm ready. Let's go.'

Ananya turned to find Arnav dressed in clean jeans and a crisp white shirt tucked neatly in. Ananya's eyebrows shot up in surprise. This was a long way from his usual scruffy T-shirt and faded jeans. For him, this was as good as black tie.

'Going somewhere special?' she asked them.

'Shopping.' Shayla beamed even as Arnav glowered.

'Shopping?' Ananya struggled to hold back the laughter bubbling in her throat as she looked at Arnav's expression. He looked miserable but determined to be brave about it.

'Shopping,' he repeated, with a tragic ring to his voice.

'Do you want to come?' Shayla asked.

Did she? Her pulse leapt at the thought of spending time with Arnav, but this was with her mother-in-law in tow.

Regretfully, she shook her head. 'I am quite tired. I'm just going to go up and sleep for a bit before dinner.'

Arnav was watching her and the look on his face had her own flaming. The depth of his love for her was both her life's most precious treasure and its most painful complication. Whenever he looked at her, she believed she was worth being loved and that she, too, deserved a happily ever after.

Shayla's phone buzzed interrupting their little moment. She stepped towards the door to take the call, leaving Arnav and Ananya in the relative privacy of the foyer.

'Long day?' he asked.

'Yes.' Ananya hefted the files under her arm. 'And it isn't over yet. I'll be working late into the night too.'

'It couldn't have helped that you didn't get much sleep last night either,' he murmured.

Ananya felt the heat rising in her cheeks again.

'Don't,' she hissed.

'Don't what, Anni? Don't remind you of the best night of my life? Don't worry about you? Don't love you?' He kept his voice low, but the emotion rang through loud and clear. 'I can't help myself when it comes to any of that, when it comes to my feelings for you.'

Her heart racing, Ananya looked over to where her mother-in-law stood. She was a few feet away chatting to someone on the phone. She loved the woman, but right now, she wished she would go away.

'Anni, I—'

Whatever Arnav was going to say was cut off by her mother-in-law's reappearance. Ananya took a conscious step back both from him and the emotion that was raking across her heart.

'Let's go,' Shayla beamed, looping her arm through Arnav's. 'Are you sure you won't join us, Ananya?'

'Come,' Arnav said. 'Please.'

Hearing that quiet plea, Ananya abandoned all her excuses. She looked at the man she'd loved for what felt like forever and knew she couldn't deny him something they both wanted and had never got enough of: some time together and the simple pleasure of each other's company.

'Okay.' She smiled at Shayla, keeping her eyes carefully averted from Arnav. 'Can you give me ten minutes to freshen up?'

Knowing something was wrong and doing it anyway definitely had to be a sin. But Ananya had already lived in hell for the last few years. Now it was time to sin enough to have deserved it and some sins were worth everything.

∽

'What's wrong with the pink one I chose?' Arnav's aggrieved question had Ananya biting her lip to keep from laughing out loud.

Exasperated, Shayla put her hands on her hips. 'It's not pink. It's mauve.'

'Call it what you want. It's still pink.'

'It's a shade of purple, you imbecile.'

Arnav raised an eyebrow at the insult. 'An imbecile you gave birth to.'

'Yes. You being colour blind is my fault,' Shayla huffed even as Ananya gave up the battle and burst into laughter.

Ignoring her, Arnav demanded, 'Why did you want me to come along if you didn't want my opinion?'

'Nobody in their right mind would want your opinion on fashion matters,' his mother retorted.

Arnav's mouth fell open. 'What's that supposed to mean?'

When both women just exchanged looks and didn't respond, he demanded an answer, 'What's wrong with the way I dress?'

'Nothing, dear. If the look you're going for is stodgy and boring, that is.'

'Stodgy? Boring?' Arnav repeated. Behind him, Ananya kept laughing like a hyena. 'You want to wear a yellow saree that makes you look like a jaundice patient, and I'm stodgy and boring?'

'This is citrine.'

'Citrine?' Thrusting his hands through his hair, Arnav prayed for patience. 'Mom, why the hell did you drag me along on this horrifying shopping trip?'

'Don't swear at your mother,' Shayla retorted primly.

'You called me an imbecile and I can't say hell?'

Ananya now had both hands on her face, but even he could see the tears of laughter streaming down her face.

'It isn't that funny,' he told her.

'It is,' she gasped even as she pressed her hand to her side. 'Believe me, it is.'

Turning his back on her, he looked at his mother, who was still draping that damn yellow saree over her shoulder and admiring herself in the mirror.

'Will you buy that damn thing already? Then we can all get out of here.' And he could have a drink.

'Maybe I should take a look at that olive green one again,' Shayla mused.

'No,' Arnav answered. 'You have seen it. You have draped it. You decided you liked this vomit-coloured one better. No going back to that green one again. Let's buy the vomit one and just leave!'

Even as he ranted, he knew he was wasting his breath. Never again would he let his mother emotionally guilt trip him into anything. Never again!

'May I help?' Ananya asked from behind him.

'No,' he told her, placing his palm on her face to gently shove her back in the chair she'd been sitting in and giggling. 'You're the one who found that vomit-coloured saree on the shelf and showed it to her. You sit there and cackle like a good little witch.'

Ananya said, 'Watch it, or I'll cast a spell on you that

you'll never be free from.'

'You already have.'

And with that, her blush was back. Forgetting for a minute that Shayla was standing a few feet away, Ananya let herself soak in the moment. She hadn't laughed this much in... she didn't know. She couldn't remember the last time she'd laughed like this.

'Arnav—'

'There you are!' Whatever she'd been about to say was drowned out by Shayla's happy exclamation.

Arnav and Ananya turned as one towards the front of the shop. As he saw the trio of women walking in and greeting his mother, he finally understood why she'd wanted him to come along. And it had nothing to do with his taste in clothes or lack thereof.

'Arnav, this is my childhood friend, Chandini. We went to school together,' his mother beamed. 'And these are her daughters, Kaajal and Chavi.'

Clasping Ananya's hand in her own, she dragged her forward. 'And this is my daughter, Ananya.'

'You're a very lucky woman, Shayla,' Chandini tittered.

Arnav felt the sudden gaze of Chandini and her daughters on him. They seemed to be assessing him. Meanwhile, standing beside him, Ananya had gone quiet. All traces of laughter and warmth were gone from her face.

'Let's all go and have coffee somewhere,' Shayla suggested as she laid a warning hand on his arm.

'I don't drink coffee,' he replied, just to be difficult.

'Then have a cup of tea,' she said, steel in her voice and gaze as she looked at him.

'I don't drink tea either,' he said, just to be perverse.

'Fine. Then take a sip from a glass of water.' She squeezed his arm in one last warning before letting go. Clapping her hands together in what he supposed was a gesture of excitement, she added, 'Let's go.'

'Not so fast,' Arnav interjected. 'Aren't you forgetting something?'

Shayla turned to look at him warily. Good, he thought savagely. She should be wary.

'You haven't bought your saree yet. Isn't that what you came for? In fact,' he turned now to include the others in the conversation, 'since we couldn't decide on a saree, maybe you could help us.'

'A man who is ready to shop. What more could a woman want?' Chandini trilled, nudging Kaajal forward. He wasn't sure whether it was Kaajal or Chavi. Frankly, he couldn't care less.

He turned to the avid salesman and said, '*Bhaiya, aur dikhaiye* (Brother, show us a few more options).'

His mother shot him a glare, to which he answered with a hard smile, 'Let's buy you something special, Mom. My treat.'

∽

An hour later, Ananya could feel the beginnings of a migraine throbbing in her head. It felt like someone was using a hammer and chisel inside her skull. Or it could just be the effect of the stupid chatter of the other women and the silent but screaming rage of the man sitting opposite from her.

She took another bracing sip of her espresso and prayed this nightmare of an evening would end soon.

'Ananya, you know what would be a great idea?' Shayla asked.

Oh shit. This was going to be far from great. 'What, Ma?' she asked obediently.

'There is a multiplex in this mall. All you kids should go watch a movie. Chandini and I will sit right here and catch up in peace.'

Next to her, Arnav sat like a furious stone statue. The man hadn't spoken a word in the last hour. The other women must have been truly idiotic to not get a hint of what he was feeling or thinking.

'Oh, that's a fabulous idea!' Kaajal squealed. Ananya winced at the sound. *Why did grown women think they had to squeal?*

'I don't know,' Ananya demurred. 'I'm really tired. Maybe the others can go. I'll just take a cab home.'

Arnav came alive at that. 'No,' he said firmly. 'I think there might be a show of that new Tom Cruise movie in the next few minutes.'

'*Top Gun?*' Chavi asked. 'I wouldn't mind watching that. Tom Cruise is my kind of man.'

'Done. Let's go.' Arnav took a hold of Ananya's arm and hauled her out of her chair. He was practically dragging her through the mall, leaving the other two girls to struggle along in their wake.

'What are you doing?' Ananya hissed.

'Watching a movie together would mean they won't be talking,' he hissed back. 'Right now, the mere idea of it sounds like heaven.'

Subsiding a little at the ire in his tone, Ananya gave up fighting her fate. She made polite conversation with the girls until Arnav bought tickets and the obligatory popcorn and cold drinks. Hustling them into the still bright theatre, he led them to their seats. They had one aisle seat followed by the other three. Before anyone could speak up, Ananya slid into the aisle seat and dumped her popcorn and Pepsi in the slots of their seat's arms.

'Chavi, come sit next to me,' she gestured the younger girl over. That would leave Kaajal and Arnav to be seated next to one another and give them the time to get to know each other, she figured, ignoring the pain that savaged her at the thought. Arnav let Kaajal sit next to Chavi and then took his seat without a word.

Ananya wondered why doing the right thing always made one so miserable. She kept her eyes resolutely fixed on the screen as the opening credits started to roll.

A few minutes later, a minor disturbance started on her right and she looked over to see Arnav slipping into Chavi's seat.

'What—'

'There's a woman in the seat next to mine who isn't comfortable with a man sitting by her side,' he cut her off before she could voice the question. He was now sandwiched between her and Kaajal. *Great!* Ananya trained her eyes back on the screen though she didn't have a clue what she was watching.

She turned her head slightly and drank in the sight of his profile in the illumination from the screen. Before she could turn away, Arnav looked down at her. In the darkened theatre, his gaze should have been unreadable, but she saw in it what should have never been there.

Arnav's hand slipped between their seats and caught her restless fingers. Twining his fingers through hers, he kept a reassuring hold on her and stared straight ahead at the screen.

It was wrong. Everything about this was wrong. But doing the wrong thing had just righted her world. Tightening her grip on his hand, Ananya held on for dear life.

Chapter 12

Arnav kept his gaze fixed on the doors that led to the operation theatre. Across from him, his father stood at the window and stared out at the view of the hospital parking lot. Next to Arnav, his mother sat, sobbing softly.

He should comfort her. He knew he should, but he couldn't bring himself to move. It should have been him. He should have been the one behind those doors. He was the bastard who'd done something wrong.

He'd sinned, there wasn't any other way to describe it, and he was the one who should have been punished. Then why was his brother the one lying unconscious on that operation table? Hadn't he been wronged enough?

The doors opened and a nurse walked out. She walked right by them without saying a word. Arnav continued to stare at the doors. They'd made them sign forms, endless forms. The doctors said there was a possibility, no, a probability that Arvin would die on the table.

Die.

Ananya was sedated and admitted in the ICU. The doctors said she was stable. He hadn't been able to see her. Only immediate family members were allowed and he wasn't one. He was no one.

She had said she was going to tell Arvin. Had she? Arnav pushed to his feet. He couldn't bear it. He couldn't bear the thought that the last thing his brother might know would be that he'd betrayed him at the basest possible level. How had this happened? How had any of this happened? How had he let it?

'Mr Saxena.' There was another doctor standing near the door. They rose as one, a united family, for once. 'We need your signature on this consent form.' He held out a clipboard. Nobody made a move to collect it. 'We need to amputate his leg. The wound is too severe and complications have set in.'

'No!' Akhilesh shouted the word. 'My son cannot be a cripple.'

'Your son will not survive without the amputation.' The steel in the surgeon's voice cut through his father's ravings.

'No!' The word was almost a scream. 'I won't sign this form. Find another way.'

'There is no other way.'

'Will either parent's signature do?' Shayla's soft voice silenced the tumult.

'Yes, Ma'am.' The surgeon glanced at her with respect in his eyes.

'I'll sign.' She took the papers, signed and handed it back without looking at anyone else.

'He'll hate you for this,' Akhilesh growled at her.

'At least, he'll be alive to hate me.'

∽

Nobody spoke on the drive home. Arnav and Shayla sat in tense silence in the front, while Ananya retreated behind the safety of her smartphone. Arnav was pretty damn sure that had he grabbed and checked her phone at that moment, the screen would have been blank.

He kept his hands firmly clenched on the steering wheel and his eyes on the darkened patch of road in front of him as they made their way through the bylanes that eventually led home. This family certainly didn't need another accident. Anger coursed through him at his mother's manipulation. He understood why she did what she did. He truly did. But she needed to understand that what she wanted was never going to happen.

The house came into view and he slowed down to allow the guards time to unlock the huge iron gates. Acknowledging their greetings with a nod, he drove past them and into the driveway.

Both Arvin and his father's cars were already parked in the garage to the left, along with the three family cars that his mother and Ananya used. Parking his car in the only vacant spot, he got out to hold the door open for his mother. She got out without a word and sailed past him with her nose in the air. She was like a queen who felt wronged in her own kingdom.

Beside him, Ananya stepped out of the car before he had a chance to open the door for her. This was the story of his life. When it came to her, he was always too late. Falling into step behind his mother, they entered the house the same way they'd made the drive home, in silence.

'One minute,' he spoke firmly, stopping his mother before she took the stairs leading up to her room. She stopped at the base with one foot on the first stair. 'I'd like to talk to you.'

Ananya moved past him. 'I should get to work or I'll be up all night. Goodnight.' The last word was uttered with a false brightness that didn't fool anyone.

'Stay,' Shayla said. 'You're family.'

Arnav saw Ananya flinch at the simple statement and knew exactly what was going through her mind. She cast one longing look at the stairs, but stayed where she was.

'Arnav can say what he wants to in front of you.' With that, Shayla led the way into the drawing room.

His mother indeed was a queen in her castle, he again thought grimly. Well, she was about to find out that this subject of hers wasn't going to take orders so easily.

'Don't ever do that again.' The words were out of his mouth before he could try and soften them.

'Don't do what?' His mother turned on him angrily. 'Don't try and find my son some happiness?'

'Happiness isn't something you shop for at the nearest fucking mall.'

'Arnav.' The distressed murmur from Ananya did nothing to calm him down.

His mother's entire body was rigid with outrage. 'Don't you dare use language like that in front of me. I raised you better than that.'

'Did you?' A bitter laugh escaped him. 'I must have missed that part because I don't remember you raising me at all. I just remember me raising myself. I'm sorry if I did such a bad job.'

Shayla reared back.

'Arnav.' Ananya was louder this time. 'Don't do this, please.'

'Why not?' he demanded. 'Why the hell not? You know what the problem in this family is? Nobody ever wants to talk about anything. And you fit in perfectly with them. You're the perfect daughter-in-law in that aspect for sure.'

Stunned at the sudden attack, Ananya took a step back from him.

Furious at himself for losing control but unwilling to stop now, he turned back to face his mother. 'You want to play mom now? Where were you when I needed you to be my mom? Where were you when I fell down the stairs and needed stitches? The driver took me to the hospital. You were at a business party with Dad. Where were you when I collapsed at school with a high fever? You were on a business trip with Dad, socializing. Where were you when Dad threw me out of the house? Where were you when I was starving in Mumbai, living off a loaf of bread for days? Where were you when I burned my hand in the restaurant so badly that I thought I'd never cook again?'

Tears welled up in his mother's eyes and spilled over. She put trembling hands to her mouth as her body shook with her sobs.

'Don't cry.' Anger draining away and leaving only hurt behind, Arnav took a step forward as Shayla took a step away from him. 'At some level, I understand. You needed to be a wife more than you could ever be a mother. I know what Dad is like. I get it. The adult in me gets it. And I know that at the bottom of it all you love me. I was grateful that at least one parent loved me.'

Shayla closed her eyes in anguish as tears continued to pour from under the closed lids.

'All I'm saying,' Arnav said in a defeated, exhausted voice, 'is please don't play mom now. Don't set me up with women for marriage. Don't tell me what to wear or what to eat. Don't interfere in my life. I like my life the way it is, Ma. Please leave me alone.'

'Why did you come back now if you feel this way about me?' Shayla's voice cracked while asking the question.

'Because I love you.' He stepped forward and enfolded her in his arms even as she struggled to pull away. 'Just as I know you love me. But it doesn't change anything I said.' He tightened his arms around her as she wept harder. 'I'll be gone soon enough and your life will go back to normal. Just let things be. Don't start trying to fix them at this point.'

'I want you to be happy,' Shayla whispered through her tears.

He met Ananya's eyes, which were shimmering with tears. 'I've never been happier.'

∽

He'd been standing at the window staring out at the night for what felt like hours when he heard a knock on his bedroom door. He knew who it was even before he hauled the door open and saw Ananya standing on the other side.

He held the door open in silent invitation and stepped back to let her pass. She slipped past him and into the room. Walking to the centre of the room, Ananya turned and waited for him to shut the door.

The door closed behind him with a soft click, leaving them facing each other in the darkness of the room. A sliver of light filtered into the room from the space beneath the shut bathroom door.

He knew she shouldn't have been there, in his room, in his life. Exhaustion crept through him as he stood there looking at her. She took up such a large part of his life and consciousness that he forgot how tiny she really was. Swamped in loose pajamas and a T-shirt that had clearly seen better days, she looked like a little girl playing dress-up in an adult's clothes. She simply stood there and stared at him. Her big, solemn eyes stared right into his soul, he thought.

She had loved him. He knew that. But he didn't know whether she still did. In the beginning, she had loved him. And it had felt so good, so right. And that's why it had destroyed him when she'd chosen to go through with the wedding and when she'd chosen Arvin over him.

In his head, he had known why and he'd understood just as he understood why his mother had always chosen his father over him, but it had still hurt like nothing before.

He'd come home for Arvin's engagement because his mother had then, like now, emotionally blackmailed him into it. It had been all about 'what will people think if you don't attend your brother's engagement?' He didn't care what people thought, but it came to matter to him because his mother was bothered by how they were perceived by others. So, he'd dragged his sorry ass home, dreading every minute of the upcoming festivities. And then he had met the bride-to-be.

'Arnav.'

Ananya's voice brought him back to the moment. Before he had a chance to refocus on the present, she stepped up and wrapped her arms around him. Arnav sighed. The stresses and worries of the day melted away along with the guilt that seemed to have become his permanent companion. In that moment, with Ananya in his arms, his world was perfect.

'You shouldn't be here.'

'No,' she agreed even as she snuggled closer. 'But I am.'

'Anni, if someone finds you here—'

'I know. I was careful.' She tipped her head back to

look at him. 'And tonight, it's not about them. For me, it's only about you.'

She stretched up to the tips of her toes to rub her nose against his in a gesture that was both tender and playful. Undone, he leaned his forehead against hers and closed his eyes.

She brushed light kisses on his shut eyelids, the tip of his nose and both cheeks until she finally reached his mouth. 'Anni,' he breathed her name like a prayer.

In response, she clutched his hair in her fist and kissed him. Content to let her take the lead, he sank into the kiss as her hands roamed gently over his back. Ananya pushed at his chest and had him falling back onto the bed. Arnav filled his hands with the soft curves of her bottom and pulled her on top of him.

He tightened his arms around her and held on. She must have sensed the quiet desperation in his embrace as she whispered, 'I'm right here.'

Yes, his mind murmured, but for how long? Squashing the thought ruthlessly, he kissed his way down her neck. He wasn't going to think of tomorrow. Tonight was about the two of them. The world and the future could wait. Ananya moaned and he forgot everything else and set himself to the task of hearing that sound more often.

Hours later, he found himself lying in bed with her cuddled up to his side. She had one leg sprawled across his waist and an arm resting against his chest. With her head on his arm, her hair strewn in a tangled mess across her face, she was fast asleep. Even as he watched her, one hand gently stroking the curve of her back, she snored a little, which left him grinning.

His grin fading, he stared out of the window to where the first rays of the sun were lightening the sky. Morning was here and with it all his doubts and misgivings. A soft touch to the side of his face had him glancing down. His lips curved at the sight of those big, serious eyes looking up into his.

'Good morning.'

'Good morning,' Ananya replied, her voice still husky with sleep. Her fingers traced the edge of his smile. 'How are you feeling?'

'Cold,' he answered honestly. 'I'd forgotten what Delhi winters are like.'

In response, Ananya cuddled up closer. She slipped her leg between his and tucked herself in as if she were a hot bottle. Ridiculously touched that she cared enough to warm him up, Arnav felt a strange burn behind his eyes. Staring hard at the ceiling above, he fought to get his emotions under control. For someone who'd been fending for himself his entire life, that simple gesture rocked his world. Last night, even if for just one night, Ananya had chosen him.

'What are we doing, Anni?' The gruff question broke the quiet of the room.

'I thought that was obvious.' Ananya laughed, but he heard the strain behind it. She sat up and pushed her hair out of her face.

Arnav didn't say a word. He just watched her. Quietly. Patiently.

'What do you want me to say?' she finally asked.

'You know what I want.' He, too, sat up, the sheet falling to pool around his waist. 'I just want to know if you want the same.'

'I'm here,' she gestured at the bed, 'with you.'

'You know what I mean, Anni.' Irritation roughened his voice.

For a moment, she didn't respond and his heart stopped only to beat again when she answered. 'I tried speaking to Arvin before he left, but the moment wasn't right.'

Arnav reached out and took her hand, twining his fingers through her cold ones. Gently stroking them to warm them, he said, 'I'm sorry, I don't mean to pressure you, but I can't share you, Anni, not anymore. You're mine.'

She looked sad. And that was not a reaction a man would like to see in response to his declaration of his undying love.

'I'm sorry,' she finally said.

'Why?' His heart clenched.

'I'm sorry for all the hurt. Your parents, Arvin, me… none of us have done right by you.'

'I don't need or want your pity.' He got off the bed in an angry gesture. Coming up from behind, she put her arms around him. When he went to remove them, she just tightened her grip and held on. His fingers curled around hers and tightened in a mute plea.

Don't pity me. Just love me. The unsaid words screamed in the silence of the room. And still she said nothing.

'Anni—' He turned around and took her face in his hand. Sacrificing his pride, he said, 'Please don't leave me.'

She pressed her soft fingers to his lips and stopped him from saying anything further. 'I'm here.' She kissed him, sweetly and softly. 'I'm right here.'

For now, it was enough. It had to be.

Happiness fizzed and bubbled inside her like champagne. For the first time in forever, Ananya was living a charmed life. Her days at the office passed in a blur, with a few minor victories in court. Her nights were the stuff fairy tales were made of.

Conscious of the fact that they couldn't be constantly seen in each other's presence in public, Ananya and Arnav met mostly within his café premises after it closed down, when the chances of anyone spotting them were practically nonexistent. The false cocoon in which they lived out their days was bright and shiny, but transient. Despite knowing that fact, which underlay everything they said or did, neither could walk away.

Ananya could see the strain etched in Arnav's face. She saw hope in his eyes when he looked at her. She knew what he wanted—a life together, one lived in the sunlight and not in the shadows. She wanted it, too. She wanted to stand by his side with pride and not skulk around behind people's backs. But fear was her constant companion. The what-ifs running through her head were driving her insane. No matter how hard she tried, Arvin always had an ace up his sleeve.

She should have taken a step back from her relationship with Arnav until she unravelled the tangled knots of her marriage and her life. She should have, but she didn't. She couldn't.

She hoarded every moment she shared with him. She planned for a future with Arnav, but deep within her lurked the frightening knowledge that fate mocked her hopes and dreams. Whether it was just her insecurities playing up or her subconscious mind warning her of things to come, she didn't know. All she knew was that this was a golden time in her life and it wouldn't last. It was just a matter of time before the other shoe dropped.

'Anni.' She snapped out of her thoughts. Arnav tapped the dish in front of her. 'Eat up. It's almost eleven and Cinderella has only an hour left.'

Ananya flushed at the Cinderella dig. Her mother-in-law had recently been getting more than a little annoyed with all the late nights Ananya had been working. She had been told to be at home latest by twelve, and if she wanted to work later than that, she could work from home.

Chafing at the unexpected curfew, Ananya twirled some spaghetti onto her fork and watched Arnav as he started to scrub the dishes he'd used to make them dinner. The muscles in his back and arms flexed as he worked.

Enjoying the view, she forked in another mouthful. As always, the food was delicious. She'd never been a huge fan of Italian food, but Arnav could drown her in olive oil and she wouldn't complain even for a second.

'Aren't you going to eat?' she asked.

'Not hungry.' Wiping dry the last dish, Arnav turned from the sink only to find Anni in front of him. Laughing, he opened his mouth and accepted her forkful of pasta. Swallowing, he deflected the next bite she tried to feed him. 'I'm really not hungry. You finish up.'

Content to watch her eat, he opened a can of Cola and sat down across from her. She worked on her laptop while he wrapped up the million odd jobs that come with opening a new venture. This was normally followed by dinner together before heading home in two different cars, with him following to make sure she was safe.

'Anni.'

Ananya felt a chill run down the back of her neck at his quiet tone. She shovelled more food into her mouth. She wouldn't have to answer if her mouth was full.

'The café is going to be ready soon. It will open in another week.'

Ananya froze. He was leaving. Panic bubbled inside her as she tried to get a grip. Swallowing her food, she faked composure. 'Congratulations! When is the opening?'

'Screw the opening,' he growled. 'I will have to get back to Mumbai and won't be able to stay here for much longer.'

Ananya's hand clenched around her fork. 'I know.'

'What happens next, Anni?'

Ananya opened her mouth, but no sound came out. 'She wet her lips and tried again. 'I—'

'I?' Arnav prompted when she stopped without saying anything else.

Ananya stood and walked over to where he sat. Stepping forward to sit in his lap, she rested her hands on his shoulders and ran her fingers through his hair.

'I'll talk to Arvin as soon as he is back. Ask for a divorce.'

'When does he get back?' Arnav asked.

'I don't know,' she shrugged. 'He doesn't keep in touch with me unless he thinks it's necessary.'

'So, we're just going to continue like this indefinitely?' The edge in his voice was unmistakable.

'No, we're not.' Temper fraying, Ananya snapped back, 'You've just informed me that you're going to pack up and leave in a week, so I obviously have a deadline to meet.'

Arnav stiffened. Pulling back from her embrace, he straightened and moved away. 'I'm sorry you feel pressured,' he said stiffly.

Keeping his back to her, he started to pack up his laptop, preparing to leave for home. 'Don't let my leaving to Mumbai push you towards anything.' Slinging his laptop bag on his shoulder, he turned, 'I've waited five years. I'm sure I can wait forever.'

Shame coursed through her at the hurt she saw darkening his eyes.

'Arnav, no,' she murmured. 'I just need a little more time. Arvin isn't going to make this easy, but I'm going to get that divorce. Regardless of whether you came back into my life or not, my marriage was anyway headed to this point. I should have taken this stand earlier, but I didn't have the courage or the strength. Now I do.'

Arnav cursed under his breath. 'I'm sorry. I swore I wouldn't pressure you, but I can't seem to help myself.'

'I'll talk to him as soon as he gets back.'

'I'd like to be there with you when you do.'

'NO!' Ananya stumbled back, her horror at the suggestion clearly visible. 'No,' she said again, less forcefully this time.

'I won't leave you to face the flak alone,' he said stubbornly.

'You can't be there.' Her panic leaked into her words. 'If he knew…'

Arnav stilled at her words. Eyes narrowed, he asked, 'What exactly are you planning to tell him?'

With a hammering heart, Ananya tried to explain. 'I'm going to ask for a divorce. He knows our marriage is a mess that can't be saved. I'm going to tell him I want out.'

'You won't tell him anything about me?' A bleak, desolate look flashed over his face.

'Not yet. Not right now. Arnav, it would destroy him.'

She begged him to understand. 'I've ruined his life once before. I don't want to do it again.'

'How does delaying it help?' he asked, his tone so cold and remote that she felt the chill in her bones.

'Time heals. It isn't just a cliché. When some time has passed, I'll tell him. We'll tell him, together,' she promised. 'That time I won't stand alone.'

'And until then?' Arnav asked. 'What kind of relationship do you see for us? This?' His hands spread out to encompass the space between them. 'Hiding from the world, pretending to be nothing more than in-laws? Fucking each other in private and smiling civilly in public?' The words were brutal, but she held her ground.

'I think we should stop.' The air seemed to go still around them. Ananya held his furious, hurt gaze. 'What we've done, no matter how we justify it, it was wrong. I want to do the rest of it right.'

'Explain.'

'We should stop seeing each other like this. You can go back to Mumbai. Meanwhile, I'll ask Arvin for a divorce. Once I'm free, then we can get back together.'

'You want me to walk away from you.' Striding forward, Arnav grabbed her arms and hauled her up against him. 'Away from this? From us?'

'Yes. But just for now, for the present.' Ananya's voice shook, but she steadied it and herself. Laying a hand against the thundering of his heart, she said, 'It would destroy you if we destroyed him.'

Arnav closed his eyes, the truth of her words striking at his heart.

'I know your family relationships are strained, but Arvin

and you have tried your best to maintain some semblance of a bond. You and I both know that hurting him is going to kill a part of you.'

'He doesn't love you.' He opened his eyes and looked down at her.

'No,' she agreed. 'But he loves *you*. Don't abandon your brother while trying to stand by me.'

Anger leached out of him, leaving only pain and fatigue behind. 'God, I hate this,' he whispered.

'I know,' Ananya whispered back. 'But this is how it has to be. I love you, Arnav. Remember that I want you, and only you.'

His arms closed around her convulsively. He held on desperately, not knowing when he would have her in his arms again.

'Just give me the time to do this right. You've waited for me this long.' She cradled his cheek in her palm. 'Won't you wait a little longer?'

Arnav gently kissed the centre of her palm. 'Be mine and I'll never ask God for anything else again.'

'I was always yours,' she vowed. 'I have never been anyone else's.'

Eyes closed, arms around each other, they tried desperately not to pretend they weren't saying goodbye. They held on tightly, but time, their enemy, slipped by, yet again.

Chapter 13

'You're leaving and...'

Ananya stood near the door to his room. His lips twisted in a bitter smile as he saw how carefully she stayed on the other side of the threshold. Arnav turned back to his suitcase and slammed it shut. Flipping the locks, he hauled it upright.

'Arnav—'

'No,' he said, 'don't.'

He looked at her standing in the doorway. Bruises bloomed on her jaw, one eye almost completely swollen shut with a horrifying black eye. She leaned a bandaged hand against the door handle to support her weakened frame.

He knew he should offer to help her, but he couldn't. He couldn't touch her.

'You should sit down,' he said gruffly.

'I will. I just wanted to say—'

'Goodbye?'

Ananya looked at him. Her other eye filled with enough pain to make his chest hurt.

'Yes,' she said finally. 'Goodbye.'

Arnav smiled, mockingly. 'Will you forgive me if I leave immediately after your wedding?'

She said nothing.

'I wish you both all the happiness in the world.' And he meant it. He wished them his share too.

'I'm sorry,' she whispered.

'Don't be. You made a choice, the right one.' He picked up his suitcase.

'Don't you want to know why?' she asked.

Arnav considered that. 'No, I don't. How does it matter? The reason will not change anything.'

'Arnav.' There was a desperate plea in her voice for forgiveness.

'Take care of him, Anni. He needs you now, more than ever.'

'And you?'

'You were never mine, Ananya.' He took a deep breath to control the tightening in his chest and prayed she'd get out of his way before he embarrassed himself.

'I'll be a good wife to him.'

There was nothing to say to that. Nothing to say to any of it. Exhausted beyond belief, Arnav said, 'I should go. I'll be back for the wedding.'

'Goodbye, Arnav.' She stepped to the side. 'Be well.'

'Bye, Anni.' He hefted his suitcase and stepped out of the room. 'Be happy.'

∽

'ARRRVINNN!'

The yelling woke up Ananya from her disturbed sleep.

'ARRRVINNN!'

The person who had been shouting his name was now getting closer to them. Disoriented and still foggy with sleep, her gaze fell on Arvin's side of the bed, which hadn't been slept in. Of course it hadn't. He wasn't in town. Shaking her head to clear it a little, Ananya swung her legs to one side of the bed and stood up just as her bedroom door was flung open.

Her father-in-law stood on the threshold with her mother-in-law hanging on to his arm as if trying to restrain him.

'Papa,' she gulped, wrapping her arms around her chest to disguise the fact that she wasn't wearing a bra.

'Where is he?' he roared, spittle flying from his lips. He looked like he was in the grip of a violent rage. Taking a step back in self-preservation, Ananya said, 'Out of town. On work.'

'Work?' Akhilesh snorted. 'That bastard doesn't have the brains to work.'

'Akhilesh,' Shayla cried, her distress evident. 'Come out. Let's go to the drawing room and talk.'

'Talk? You want to talk?' For a moment, it looked like he would strike her, but he pushed past her and stormed away from the open doorway. Grabbing the robe thrown over the back of a chair, Ananya followed, more for Shayla's protection than for any desire to be in the middle of a family dispute.

Akhilesh went straight to the bar and poured himself a hefty dose of Scotch. Gulping it down in one go, he shrugged off the calming hand Shayla placed on his shoulder.

'What happened?' she asked, her tone low and conciliatory. 'Whatever it is, I'm sure we can find a solution.'

'You're sure, are you?' he sneered in response.

Arnav entered the room quietly and went to stand behind his mother.

'The prodigal son returns,' Akhilesh sneered again. Ananya hadn't realized until that moment how most of her father-in-law's expressions swung between contempt, disdain, anger and boredom.

'You know what, all of this is your fault,' he gestured towards Shayla with his whiskey, sloshing more than half of it over the rim. 'You gave me two sons. The older one has the brains and all the business acumen you could ask for, but all he wants to do is be a bloody woman. A cook. Bloody waste of space,' he spat the words out.

'The younger one doesn't have the brains of a fucking flea. Good-for-nothing fucking cripple.'

The sheer depth of vitriol had Ananya gasping. She opened her mouth to say something, but Shayla spoke up instead. 'Don't say that. Arvin has done everything possible to make you happy. He works so hard and does everything just the way you want it. He's spent his life being a good son to you. Why can't you be proud of him?'

At this, Ananya wondered whether Shayla even realized she hadn't bothered to defend Arnav at all. Ananya looked at Arnav, but he showed no reaction to either parent's words. His face completely devoid of expression, he watched the interaction between his parents.

'Proud of him? Proud?' Akhilesh looked like he might have a stroke. Reaching over, he grabbed the pearl necklace around Shayla's neck and pulled it from her neck. The fragile piece gave way and pearls rained down around them as Shayla gave a distressed cry.

Ananya and Arnav both moved to stand between the two of them. Unconsciously ranging themselves shoulder to shoulder, they kept Shayla out of his reach as she started to sob behind them. Akhilesh scooped up a fistful of pearls and threw it at their faces.

'Stop crying over your jewellery. It's all going to go away,' he said.

'What do you mean?' Arnav asked. Those were the first words he'd spoken since he'd entered the room.

'Your brother has ruined us.' The words dropped like stones into the room, broken only by Shayla's soft weeping.

'Define ruined,' Arnav said evenly.

'We're bankrupt. He's dropped us in such a deep hole, that we can never climb out of it.'

'That's not true!' Shayla retorted. 'It cannot be.'

'Yes. It is.'

The family turned as one to see Arvin standing at the entrance to the drawing room.

'It's true, Ma.' Arvin left his suitcase propped up against the door and stepped forward. 'I screwed up.' He held his father's gaze and said, 'I'm sorry.'

'Sorry?' Akhilesh's eyes bulged. 'You're sorry?'

He suddenly moved towards Arvin, but Arnav was faster. He took the blow meant for his brother without even blinking. The slap on Arnav's cheek seemed to paralyse the rest of the room. Arnav's head swung to one side, his cheek reddening with the force of the blow. When he straightened, Ananya saw his lip was bleeding. A soft sound of distress escaped her before she could control it, but she did not catch anyone's attention.

Wiping the blood trickling down his chin, Arnav calmly faced his father like nothing had happened. Arvin stood at his back. Shayla continued to weep in the background, but no one seemed to notice.

'You think being sorry makes it okay?' Akhilesh asked, the venom in his tone had Ananya bracing for more violence. She wondered whether she should call the cops before the situation escalated.

'No, but I don't know what else I can say,' Arvin shrugged helplessly. 'What can I say to make it okay?'

'I gave you everything on a platter. All you needed to do to succeed was keep things going as they were, but you aren't capable of even that. Bloody failure! You should have died in that accident.'

'I wish I had,' Arvin said sounding defeated.

Outrage churned through Ananya. She felt sorry for the two brothers, who had such parents—an abusive tyrant for a father and a weak mother. Her heart broke as she saw the brothers facing them, Arnav still shielding Arvin the best he could.

'No.' The firm rebuttal broke through Ananya's mental turmoil. Deliberately turning his back on his father, Arnav faced Arvin.

Grabbing his brother's face between his palms, he repeated. 'No. You don't ever say that again. Rule of thumb. Anything that comes out of that man's mouth is not worth paying attention to.'

'Touching.' Akhilesh clapped his hands slowly. 'This brotherly love is very touching, but how is it going to be of any help? We're going to be out on the streets if we don't find a way out of this mess.'

Arnav looked at Arvin and said, 'I'll fix it.' When Arvin shook his head in denial, he gripped his neck and made him meet his eyes. 'Trust me, I will.'

Arvin nodded, looking lost and helpless. Ananya had never seen him like that. He'd always been this huge, overpowering figure in her life. To see him so low, so broken…it hurt her. She watched from the side as a single tear rolled down his cheek. She watched as his elder brother drew him into an embrace that seemed to be the only thing holding him up and keeping him from falling apart.

'Fucking loser.' With the muttered abuse, Akhilesh swept out of the room.

Shayla stood up slowly, her age evident in every movement. She stopped for a second to run a hand gently over Arvin's hair and then she hurried after her husband.

'I don't know how you're going to fix this, Bhai,' Arvin said. 'I've been over everything with a fine-tooth comb in the last ten days and I just can't find a way.'

She could see that even Arnav didn't have a clue what he was going to do, but he seemed determined to try. 'There's always a way. We just have to look hard enough.' He looked over Arvin's shoulder at Ananya and tried to smile, but the cut in his lip had him wincing. 'We'll do it. Together.'

∽

'Do you have anything to drink?' Arvin asked, not looking at him once they reached Arnav's room.

'Not here. I can get you a beer from the kitchen if you want?' Arnav offered.

Arvin nodded and Arnav left to grab the beers from the kitchen. His mind whirling, he rummaged through the drawers for a bottle opener. Not finding anything, he gave up and resorted to a trick they'd learned in their college days. Angling the bottle, he used his teeth and opened both beers before heading back upstairs.

Handing one bottle over to Arvin, he sat down across from his brother. They could start discussing their family business affairs later. Now was the time to talk about the greater mess at hand, which was their family.

'Nothing's changed, has it?' Arvin brooded as he sipped from his bottle. 'Dad, Mom, you, me…we're all still stuck in this same unhealthy, abusive rut.'

'You can get out of it anytime you want,' Arnav said. 'I did. It wasn't easy, but it's doable.'

'That's exactly what I was trying to do by expanding internationally. I wanted to get out and away from this family and this miserable life. I wanted a new life in a new country with a business I would have grown from scratch.' He started picking at the label on the bottle, peeling it away. 'I guess I just wanted what you have.'

The irony of the last statement slammed into Arnav like a sledgehammer. He'd spent the last five years desperately wanting what Arvin had and it turned out that his brother had been feeling the same way.

He watched as the label came apart under Arvin's restless fingers and fell on the bed in shreds. Even if he tried, Arnav knew he wouldn't be able to put it back together on the bottle, just like he couldn't fix the business and make it what it was. Though he had told his brother he would fix everything, he wasn't sure how he would. And how was he ever going to fix the larger betrayal Arvin didn't even know about yet.

'She's going to leave me.'

Heart sinking, Arnav took in the sight of his brother slumped against the headboard of the bed. He looked lost and vulnerable.

'Ananya is going to leave me.' Arvin laughed mirthlessly. 'Isn't that just the icing on the cake? That ties up all the loose ends. The business, money, reputation, it's all gone. After she leaves, I'll have nothing left to lose.'

Arnav chose his words carefully. 'I was under the impression that you weren't happy in your marriage.'

'Is it possible to be happy with someone who wishes you were someone else?'

Arnav could feel his world starting to collapse around him. He could feel his chest tightening. He mustered up the strength to ask, 'Do you love her?'

'As much as I hate her.' Arvin shut his eyes, missing the devastated look on his brother's face. 'I accidentally crashed the car when she told me she was in love with someone else and didn't want to marry me.' 'Crashed the car,' he repeated, 'and lost my leg. She married me then.' Arvin smiled, a bitter, twisted grimace. 'She married me out of guilt and because she felt responsible for what happened to me.'

'Why did you marry her?' Arnav forced the question out.

'Because I loved her and I thought maybe over time she would love me, too. But it didn't work out that way. All she feels looking at me is guilt, shame and a healthy dose of pity.'

'And what do you feel for her now?' He had to know because it would change everything.

'I resented her all these years and did everything I could to push her away. Every time I looked at her, she reminded me of what I'd lost in that one night…her and myself in more ways than one.' He knocked a hand against the prosthetic, the noise ringing through the otherwise quiet room. 'I treated her like crap, Bhai, but she still stuck around. She didn't leave me. And now…'

'And now?' Despite knowing the answer, he still asked the question.

'Now, she will. She didn't leave me then, but she didn't love me either. She still loves the other guy, whoever he is. The lucky bastard.'

Bastard, yes, Arnav thought. The luck part was debatable, but he was a bastard, through and through.

∽

Ananya couldn't sleep. The two brothers were huddled together in Arvin's room while going over the whole mess and trying to sort through the tangle of the business's prospects. In her own room, she stepped out onto her balcony and looked up at the moon. The full moon hung low and round, spreading enough light for her to look out onto the vista of buildings spread out in front of her.

She couldn't get over the events of the evening and how quickly things had changed. Though she had woken up from the nightmare that plagued her sleep, she had a feeling that her current nightmare wasn't something she would be getting rid of very easily.

Arnav had asked her to trust him and she did, but if things were as bad as they sounded, could he really find a way around it? And what would happen if he couldn't?

A sound had her turning. She watched Arvin enter the room and leave his suitcase by the bed. Exhaustion and pain lined his face. Dropping to his side of the bed, he pulled his trouser leg up and removed his prosthetic. He leaned forward and dug his fingers into the ruined flesh, massaging it in hope of relief.

Ananya stepped into the room. She didn't meet his gaze as she reached for the balm he kept in the corner of his table. Picking it up, she held it out to him. After a moment of silence, Arvin took it. His fingers fumbled a little with the lid, but he managed to open it. Just when he was about to scoop up some of the ointment, the bottle slipped from his fingers, bounced on the floor and rolled under the bed.

'Bloody hell.' He fell back on the bed and closed his eyes. When he didn't move for a while, Ananya bent forward and retrieved the balm. Arvin hadn't moved an inch and still had his eyes closed.

Slipping two fingers into the cool ointment, Ananya slowly started to smear it over the red, puckered flesh around the stump of his leg. It was the first time she'd touched it. Arvin had shunned the initial attempts she had made to care for him and eventually she had stopped trying.

She didn't look up even though she could feel Arvin's gaze on her. She massaged the stump the best way she could until she heard him exhale in relief. When she was done, she stood and capped the bottle before placing it back on the table.

'Why?' he asked quietly.

Ananya didn't pretend not to understand. 'Because I wanted to.'

'Because you feel sorry for me?' He sat up and faced her. 'Do you know what it does to a man to live with pity, shame and guilt? Every single day? Especially when none of those are his own emotions.'

Ananya flinched. 'I'm sorry.'

'So am I,' he said it so quietly that she almost didn't hear it. Standing on his good foot, he hopped past her and into the bathroom. She sat on the side of the bed and stared at the shut bathroom door. After a few minutes, it opened again and Arvin made his way back to the bed. The pained hobble had her averting her gaze, so she didn't cause him any more discomfort than he already felt.

'Your father is wrong,' she said as he sat on his side of the bed. 'You're not a failure.'

'And yet you love another man.' Arvin laughed, the bitter sound of it had her flinching. 'Nothing makes a man feel less of a man than knowing his woman wants someone else.'

'I can't help how I feel,' she whispered, keeping her eyes trained on the wall in front of her.

'No,' he agreed. 'Neither can I.'

They sat in silence for a while longer, neither moving nor speaking.

'You're leaving me, aren't you?' Arvin asked, his voice hollow and devoid of all emotions. Ananya looked up from where she'd been staring at the bedsheet. He was watching her carefully. 'I've known since the night you refused me in the bathroom. You've never said no before.'

No, she never had. She'd hated every minute of it, but she'd done what she'd perceived was the right thing. She'd done her best to be a good wife.

'You don't want me,' she said avoiding, for the moment, the direct question he'd asked. 'You hate me.'

'Hate is a strong word.'

A disbelieving laugh escaped her. 'Arvin, you've done everything possible to make me miserable over the years.'

'Yes,' he accepted readily. 'I did. I was hurting and I wanted you to hurt, too.'

'You don't hurt anymore?' she asked, still unable to believe they were actually having this conversation.

'I'm tired, Ananya.' He let his head fall back against the bedrest. 'I'm so tired. I think I may be too tired to feel any hurt.' After another beat of silence, he said, 'I won't fight you. Not anymore. If you want a divorce, you can have it.'

Her throat clogged with emotion. Everything she'd wanted was within her grasp. All she had to do was reach out and grab it.

Arvin pushed himself to a sitting position again. With a curse, he reached for the painkillers he had stashed in the bedside table and took one. He slumped forward and rested his head in his hands, massaging his temples slowly.

'We used to be friends once,' she said finally. 'Could we…'

'No,' he said. 'This is not about forgiveness or absolution. If you're going, just get out. We're not friends and we can't be friends. I don't want to see your face again after the divorce.'

With that, he stood and shuffled towards the bathroom door again, one hand on the wall for leverage. The door shut firmly in her face seconds later.

∽

Arnav was wading through the business's legal and financial papers when he heard a knock on the door. He knew who it was even before he answered. Pain knifed through him when he realized what was coming, but he walked forward and opened the door nevertheless. Ananya stepped past him and into the room.

Shutting the door, Arnav turned to find her studying the papers strewn all over the bed.

'Ananya.'

She stiffened, a small part of her mind noting she was Ananya again and not Anni for him.

'Let me take a look at these? I could help.'

Without waiting for an answer, she sat down and started going through them one at a time. Arnav took his place and continued with what he had been doing before she had arrived. They worked side by side in silence, sorting, sifting and finally making notes of action points.

Ananya had all the legal notices to her left and was working her way through the pile when she found one document.

'Arnav,' she said, speaking for the first time since entering the room, 'Have you seen this?'

Arnav took the paper she held out to him and read it. Frowning, he said, 'I can understand why Arvin ignored it. Our father would have had a fit had he even suggested it.'

Ananya pointed out, 'Faced with bankruptcy, he might have a different view.'

Arnav had to concede the point. 'Arvin didn't even mention it. I'll check with him what the exact terms of the offer were.'

Ananya took the paper back and read through it again. It was an offer to merge the hotel chain with a larger corporate. There was also a covering letter from her father explaining and simplifying the legalese of it. It would mean the Saxenas would have to sell their stake and relinquish all control over the business. They would still have a seat on the board, but the controlling power and interest would no longer be theirs. They would be mere figureheads, if that.

Her father, she noticed, strongly advised against the Saxenas accepting the offer. It had been a wrong call and she was more than a little surprised seeing that her father had made it. She wanted to believe that he must have known about the state of the business as their legal head.

'You realize what it means if this goes through?' she asked, her mind still whirling with all the possibilities.

'Arvin would be free of Dad and the business.' Arnav rose from the bed and walked over to the window. He seemed to spend a lot of time gazing out into the darkness. 'He would be able to do whatever he wants and live the life he always wanted.'

Ananya stared at the paper as if it held the answers to all the mysteries of the universe. In some ways, it held the answers to her universe. 'I don't think he even knows what he wants.'

That was true, Arnav supposed, but his brother deserved the chance to find out. A chance that Arnav had stolen from him the day he'd walked out. It wasn't the only thing Arnav had stolen. His gaze went to the woman sitting opposite him, studying the papers that would eventually pave the way for the end of their relationship.

It was the only way out. He wished he could find another solution, but even just a cursory glance at the company's financials told him Arvin had hopelessly overextended himself. He'd been robbing Peter to pay Paul for so long, he had long since lost sight of firm ground.

There was nothing left to do but sell the business, either as a whole, as was suggested in the letter of intent Ananya was holding, or in pieces. It would mean a drastic comedown in the lifestyle his family enjoyed, but at least they wouldn't be out on the streets.

They'd just have to get used to living like normal folks.

They'd have to get used to living like him. A small laugh escaped him at the thought. His father despised the way Arnav lived his life. Contempt for his tiny, two-bedroom apartment in Mumbai and the simple lifestyle he lived dripped from every word Akhilesh spoke about it.

There really was no option other than selling the business. But it was going to be a battle to convince Akhilesh Saxena. His father's ego would blind him to what was conceivably the only solution left.

'Arnav,' the worry in Ananya's voice wrenched him from his thoughts, 'this offer was time bound.'

Dread gnawed at his stomach. 'When did it end?'

'Two weeks ago.'

'That's not long back.' He dragged a hand through his hair. 'I can restart the conversation and see if we can bring them back to the table. It will probably mean taking a hit in the buyout, but I don't see any other way around that.'

'A radical drop in the amount means not being able to cover all the loans,' Ananya pointed out. 'What if we asked for other bids? Put the word out that Ariaa is up for sale and see who offers the most? What if we sell one hotel and keep the others?'

'If it's perceived as a distress sale, we'll be lucky if we get peanuts. I'm sure word is out in the market about our financial problems. These guys obviously saw the opportunity before the others did and swooped in for the kill.'

'We might attract other buyers if they perceive us as receptive to offers. We could at least give it a shot.'

'And if that shot fails and we have to go back crawling to these guys, they'll offer us nothing,' Arnav replied. 'This is our best bet.'

'Gamble a little,' Ananya urged.

'Not with their lives. I would and have with mine, but not with theirs.' He shook his head. 'I just need to get them back on stable ground again and then—'

He stopped himself before he could say anything more.

'And then you can leave,' Ananya finished for him. She saw the writing on the wall. She saw it in the way he held himself, in the way he hadn't touched her since she'd entered. Not once.

Guilt joined the dread still swirling inside him. 'I was always scheduled to leave after the opening of the new café.'

'Yes,' she said, staring at him. 'You were.' It felt like she could see into his heart, that wretched, scarred mockery of an organ.

'Ananya—'

'I know.' A sad, little smile played on her lips. 'I know.'

She was Ananya again. It was funny how the sound of her name could hurt so much.

'He loves you.' The words ravaged his heart, leaving it raw and bloody. 'I didn't know.'

'Does he?' Her smile disappeared. 'I haven't seen any evidence of it in all these years.'

'He told me himself.' Arnav's throat felt like it was scraped raw, every word he forced out raking fresh claws against it.

'So you decided to return me to him, like a package or a toy that you're no longer interested in?' Bitterness welled inside her. She should have known. How could she have not known it would end like this?

'I thought—' Arnav cut himself off. How did it matter what he thought?

Ananya stared over his head at the wall behind him, a

faint sheen of moisture in her eyes. He wanted to fall to his knees and beg for forgiveness. He wanted to grab her and hold on forever. He wanted to take her hand and walk out of this house. Instead, he kept his voice even as he said, 'Could you please look at me?'

She looked at him with a broken heart. He was all she'd ever wanted. She loved every inch of him so dearly. And he was the only thing God and fate had consistently denied her—God, fate and her own choices.

'He won't survive losing you.' His words sounded faint, like they were coming from a distance.

She blinked back the tears and took a deep breath. 'But you will.'

He already had once before. She believed he hadn't just survived, he'd thrived. Pain shattered her from the inside, but she hid it. His silence being her only answer, she stood and faced him. If not anything else, she would hold onto her pride and self-respect. The Saxena brothers would not have that.

'Are you going to leave him?'

'I don't believe that's any of your business anymore.' The words were calm, her voice steady.

He took the blow without flinching. They stared at each other for a moment.

'Goodbye, Arnav,' she finally said. The words were soft, but they lanced through him, leaving a burning trail in its wake.

'Goodbye, Anni.'

'Ananya,' she reminded him. 'Ananya Arvin Saxena.'

She left without a backward glance. The door shut behind her with a quiet click that reverberated in the silent room.

'Goodbye, Anni,' he whispered again. 'Be well. Be happy.'

Chapter 14

'Security!'

The shout woke up Ananya. Disoriented, she struggled to her feet from the uncomfortable chair she had dozed off in. She was in Arvin's hospital room and he was the one shouting. A portly guard in uniform burst through the door and panted to a stop.

'Sir, kya hua? *(Sir, what happened?)*'

'Throw her out. I don't want her to be allowed inside my room again.'

Confused, the man looked at Ananya. 'But aapki biwi hain na, Sir? *(But, isn't she your wife, Sir?)*'

An incoherent growl of fury erupted from Arvin and had Ananya and the guard backing away from the bed.

'Aap jaiye, bhaiya *(You can leave),*' Ananya said quietly, holding Arvin's hate-filled gaze with her own steady one. 'Mein manage kar loongi *(I'll manage on my own).*'

'You're not my wife,' he snarled the moment the door shut behind the security guard.

'Not yet,' she agreed.

'And never will be.'

Ananya didn't respond to that.

'Is there anything I can do for you?' she asked.

'Haven't you done enough already?' The rage had eked out, leaving only weariness behind. *'God, my head hurts...'*

Without another word, she came to sit next to him on his bed. Her cool, soft fingers started to massage his temples in slow, rhythmic motions.

'That won't help,' he said even as the pain ebbed a little.

'I know,' she answered.

'You shouldn't be here.'

'I know.'

'You're not my wife,' he said again.

'I know.'

'I hate you, Ananya.' The words were barely a whisper.

'I know.'

∽

Ananya lifted her glass of white wine and took another desultory sip. She watched as the glittering throng of people drifted from one group to another making business deals or exchanging gossip. It was the fortieth wedding anniversary party of a CEO and a fashion designer-cum-socialite. A match made in heaven indeed.

She was probably one of the few people who noticed that the couple never spoke directly to each other. In fact, their expressions grew tight and pinched every time they had to address each other. If that was what forty years of wedded bliss looked like, she was going to need more alcohol.

She sipped again wondering if she had really emptied the entire bottle of wine, and whether it would fill the emptiness inside her. Maybe she needed another bottle.

He was gone. The company sold. She'd moved with her

in-laws and husband to a modest three-bedroom apartment in an upper middle-class neighbourhood. She'd embraced her new lifestyle with an enthusiasm markedly missing in the other three.

She felt free. She felt calm. She felt normal. No more pretentions, no more business associates to impress. She was an ordinary woman who worked at a job she loved and went back to a family and home she did her best by. It was enough. Whenever the image of a lean, laughing face flashed before her eyes, she closed them and willed it away. It had to be enough.

It had been a month since Arnav had left. He'd stayed to attend backbreaking meetings with lawyers and accountants, for acquisition meetings, for not only finding them a new home but also for helping them make the transition. He'd stayed for his father's rage, for his mother's hysteria and for his brother's depression. But he hadn't stayed for her.

From the moment Ananya had walked out of his bedroom, she'd ceased to exist for him. He, too, should have ceased to exist for her. She was failing at her end of the bargain.

She missed him with an ache in her heart that never seemed to go away. She wanted desperately to move on, to stop thinking about him, to start feeling better, but in the end, all she wanted was him. She knew in her heart that he would never come back again, neither for her nor for his family.

'Ananya.' Arvin's voice cut through her thoughts. 'You should probably go easy on that.' He tipped his head towards the wine glass.

Arvin and she had finally arrived at a comparatively peaceful stage in their relationship, no matter how fragile or tentative. She wouldn't claim their marriage was a happy one, but they weren't hurting each other anymore. They'd even managed to spend a couple of cordial evenings together.

Ananya took another sip of the wine. It burned a fiery trail down her throat. Somedays, the urge to confess everything to Arvin consumed her. But the memory of what happened the last time she'd come clean stopped her.

Barely suppressing a shudder, Ananya emptied her glass. At the rate she was going, she was well on her way to becoming an alcoholic.

'Why don't we get some fresh air?' In one smooth motion, Arvin had her out of her chair, away from the bottle she was reaching for and walking towards the huge French doors that opened out on the adjoining terrace.

She stepped out onto the marbled terrace and took a deep breath. A second later, she doubled over with a coughing fit that had her chest heaving and her eyes watering. Someone was burning garbage in the open plot next door and she'd got a lungful of the smoke with that deep breath of 'fresh air'.

'Shit.' She heard Arvin mutter as he patted her ineffectively on her back. 'This was a bad idea.'

'It's okay,' Ananya gasped, straightening the rose-coloured linen dress he was unintentionally crumpling with his attempts at comforting her. 'I'm okay.'

Arvin steered her to the other end of the terrace where the air was relatively cleaner. The corner they stood in was wreathed in darkness, the only illumination being the muted glow from the distant lights of the party going on inside.

Ananya leaned against the balustrade and stared up at the night sky. Not a star in sight. No sign of the moon either. The sky was an inky, ominous black.

Arvin rested his back on the marble pillar next to them

and watched her. 'Looking for a shooting star?'

'I'm sorry?' Startled, Ananya turned to look at him. 'A shooting star? I didn't know you believed in stuff like that.'

'I don't, but you do.'

'I used to,' Ananya corrected. 'I don't believe in anything anymore.'

Silence greeted that pronouncement. After a moment, Arvin asked, 'If you could have anything in the world or be anything in the world, what would it be?'

'Anni,' Ananya answered without thinking. 'I'd want to be Anni.'

'You want to be called Anni?' Arvin asked with a frown.

'No.' Wine loosening her tongue, she answered, 'I want to *be* her.'

After a beat of silence, Arvin asked, 'And who is Anni?'

'Anni is loved,' she replied, staring up at the starless sky. She would have said more, but someone called out to them. They turned as one to watch one of Arvin's friends walk towards them.

'Can't you keep the romancing for home? This is a party, man. Let's go and have some fun.'

Ananya didn't protest as Arvin was towed away. All she felt was relief as she watched him leave. The relief was echoed on his face, too. They were trying to maintain a semblance of normalcy in their married life, but after so many years of bitterness and anger, it was hard work.

She turned away again and stared into the endless dark of the night. She wondered what Arnav was doing, if he ever thought of her, whether he was working in his kitchen at this moment, shouting orders at his assistants. She loved how he looked in his chef's whites—calm, confident and controlled.

A loud shout from the party indoors broke her reverie. Sighing, she moved towards the brightly lit doors. She should go in or people would come looking for her. If not for anything else, there was a wine bottle with her name on it. She would go in for that.

ഗ

Arvin was having a blast with his friends. Guiltily checking on Ananya, occasionally, to make sure she did not want anything, he escaped to the bar and the raucous partying that was going on around it.

The complete lack of connect between them bothered him. He had assumed that when they both decided to let go of their anger and pain, they would be able to forge a strong bond. Apparently, his assumptions had been wrong. He did notice the relief on Ananya's face when he'd been called away by his friend and he couldn't even resent it because that's what he felt, too.

Listening with half an ear to his friend talk about the woman he was dating, he signalled to the bartender to get him another drink. He picked up the whiskey glass set in front of him and took a big gulp.

Another glance over his shoulder told him Ananya was making fast work of the wine in her glass. He sighed. They should leave before either of them made an ass of themselves in front of the who's who of the high society they mingled in. His family had barely been able to live down the scandal of losing their business. His mother had gone into social hibernation and it was quite possible his father was in depression. But no one was brave enough to suggest that maybe Akhilesh

Saxena needed to see a doctor.

A familiar guilt slid through him. He was responsible for the entire mess and for what his family was going through. But while everyone else was losing it, Arvin found himself with a strange sense of newfound freedom. It was like a weight had been lifted off his shoulders and he had his brother to thank for it.

Arnav had fought like a demon for Arvin's chance to be set free. He'd confronted their father, consoled their mother, closed the deal with the company buying them out before anyone could have second thoughts.

His phone rang at that moment and he pulled it out of his pocket to check who it was. He grinned when he saw it was Arnav. It was almost like he'd conjured him up.

'Bhai,' Arvin said in greeting. 'How are you?'

'Good. And you?'

'As good as can be.' He took another sip from his glass.

'You're at a party, it seems,' Arnav said, hearing the loud chatter and noises around Arvin. 'I'll call some other time.'

'No.' Arvin was already moving away from the bar. 'It's nothing important. Keep talking. I'm on my way out of the room.'

He stepped out onto the terrace again. 'So, how's Mumbai?'

'Good.' Arnav's reply was terse. His brother was always curt and terse nowadays as if someone had surgically removed his smile and sense of humour. 'How is everyone?'

Arvin responded like he always did, 'Mom spends a lot of time in the puja room crying. Dad is still brooding in the bedroom. They both refuse to come out and meet people. I think we need to stage some kind of intervention there.'

Arnav didn't seem to appreciate his flippant tone. 'Give

them some time. Their lifestyle has, after all, undergone a drastic change.'

His guilt was back. 'I know. It's just...' he raked his hands through his hair in frustration, '...they aren't even willing to try.'

'Mom will when Dad does.'

And wasn't that the story of their lives. Arvin often wondered why his parents had even bothered to have kids. They were so engrossed in their own lives that they would have been better off not having any. Squashing the errant thought, he refocussed on the conversation.

'And how are you?' Arnav asked again.

Arvin was tempted to be flippant again but stopped. 'I don't know.'

'You have to stop blaming yourself.'

'Who should I blame, if not myself?' Arvin countered. 'Everything that's happened is directly my fault and no one else's.'

'Arvin.' Arnav's sigh could be heard loud and clear over the phone. In the background, Arvin heard someone call out to his brother.

'You should go. It sounds like you're busy.' Not like he was busy or going to be busy, Arvin thought. His life was stretched out endlessly in front of him with nothing to fill all the free time. It didn't help that his wife was a complete workaholic. He sat in bed every day with a mug of tea watching her get ready and run out the front door. As he held the phone, he could hear the clatter and shouts of the busy kitchen behind Arnav.

Arvin envied the two of them. He envied their passion, their drive, their busy and complete lives. He, on the other hand, had nothing.

Arnav wrapped up a brief conversation with the person in the background and was back on the line.

'I have a few more minutes,' Arnav said. 'Have you given any more thought to what you want to do?'

He'd given a lot of thought to it, but there wasn't much for someone his age to do. He couldn't, for instance, become a doctor now, at the age of thirty.

'Arvin.' Arnav's impatient voice cut through his mental rambling. 'Are you there?'

'Yes,' he cleared his throat. 'I have been thinking about it, but I haven't come up with anything yet. Do you have any ideas?'

'I have lots of ideas, but this is about what you want, not what anybody else wants for you.'

He panicked. He didn't know what he wanted. He had spent his entire life fulfilling his father's dreams. He had never had the time to come up with a dream of his own. The only thing he wanted was to fly, which was a dream unattainable for obvious reasons.

'You could still brainstorm with me, right?' he asked his brother.

'Of course,' Arnav replied. 'Why don't we talk in the morning? I'll call you around eleven. Does that time work?'

Any time worked, Arvin thought dryly. Staring at the wall, watching television, eating junk food pretty much formed his busy schedule for every day. But all he said aloud was, 'Sure, that works.'

Another shout in the background had Arnav turning away from the phone and yelling back. Arvin waited patiently for him to return to the call.

How times had changed. There was a time his brother and

he were barely speaking with one another. Their relationship had been fraught with the underlying tension between Arnav and their father, and Arvin had subconsciously, if not overtly, picked a side: his father's, the wrong one. Knowing that maintaining a good relationship with his brother would strain the one with his father, he'd picked the path of least resistance and had only a surface relationship with Arnav.

The same brother from whom he had turned away was the one who stood by him now. The father he'd lived his life for had turned his back on him in a heartbeat.

God, he was a loser. He couldn't even figure out what he wanted to do on his own. He was waiting for his big brother to come up with a plan while he sat around drowning in self-pity and guilt.

Arnav came back on the line. 'I have to go now. I'll call in the morning and we'll chat some more.'

'Actually, I do have an idea,' Arvin blurted out. It wasn't a structured business plan, and was more of a germ of a thought as of now.

'I'm listening.'

Arnav's calm voice gave him the courage to articulate what was swirling through his head. 'I would like to start an HR agency that specializes in placing differently abled people in renowned companies.'

'That sounds…' Arnav's voice trailed off.

Sounds what? Idiotic? Impulsive? Useless? Arvin could end that sentence in a dozen different ways.

'Interesting,' Arnav said. 'Really interesting.'

'Really?' Arvin questioned with a smile.

'Yes. Really. We'll talk some more when I call in the morning.'

'Okay.' Arvin was glad no one was around to see the foolish grin on his face. He was glad he had something to look forward to, something that excited him.

'So, how's everyone coping?' Arnav asked again.

Frowning, Arvin answered, 'You already asked me that and I told you. Mom and Dad are hibernating at home. I'm doing okay.'

'And?'

'And what?' Arvin tried not to sound cranky. He wasn't sure what Arnav wanted to know.

'And how is Anni doing?'

'Who?'

'Your wife, dumbass. How is your wife doing?'

'Oh, her,' Arvin flushed. He'd forgotten all about her. 'She's absolutely fine. She gets up in the morning, dashes off to work, comes home just in time for our awfully stilted family dinners. In fact, I think she might be preferring our new life to the old one.'

'Good.' Arnav was back to sounding clipped and crabby. 'It's good she's happy.'

'Oh, she seems very happy.' Arvin couldn't keep himself from sounding bitter. 'She just seems to be drinking a bit too much. Drowning her sorrows or celebrating her happiness, I'm not too sure.'

'What do you mean by drinking too much?' Arnav sounded tense.

Arvin shrugged. 'She's on her fourth glass of wine right now and she looks like she's aiming to finish her second bottle.'

'But you said she was happy.'

'She is, I think,' Arvin shrugged again. 'I don't know. I haven't asked her directly.'

'Then ask,' Arnav snapped. 'Who doesn't ask his wife if she's happy or not?'

'Almost all husbands,' Arvin replied dryly. 'That's a loaded question to ask your wife, Bhai.'

When his brother didn't answer, he continued, 'I'm sure she's happy. She's got her work to keep her going and Ananya never did care about anything beyond that. The parties, the lifestyle, the image, the expectations…she would have been happy if they'd never existed in the first place.'

'Good.' For some reason, Arnav sounded as despondent as he felt. 'I'm glad. I really have to go now. Talk soon.'

Arvin kept his phone back in his pocket and looked out at the outlines of the huge trees that lined the hotel grounds. They looked ominous in the pitch dark of the night.

An HR agency for the differently abled. He felt a prickle of excitement course through him at the mere thought of it. It would be challenging, interesting and, most importantly, it would make a difference in many people's lives.

A particularly loud cheer from the party had him glancing back. It was time to go home. He wanted to think this through and start doing some research into the idea. He wanted the quiet of home and his trusty laptop.

Something niggled at the back of his mind. He felt like he'd just heard something important, but he couldn't for the life of him figure out what it was. Unable to put his finger on it, he pushed back from the balustrade. Whatever it was, it would come to him.

He turned to face the hall and realized he could see Ananya clearly from where he stood. She was sitting with an elderly couple, a polite smile pasted on her face as she nodded in response to what they were saying.

She looked poised, groomed and beautiful in her classic linen dress. He wished he could break the ice between them and have a chance at living a life similar to the one shared by the grey-haired couple. He started walking towards their table when it hit him.

How is Anni? he'd asked. *Anni.*

Chapter 15

Penance. The concept was both fluid and relative.

Ananya kept her eyes straight ahead as she walked around the havan kund. Family and friends gave them their blessings showering handfuls of rice and flower petals on them. Close to a thousand people had come to attend their wedding.

Behind her, Arvin stumbled. He was still getting used to the crutches. Ananya turned and caught him before he fell. Glancing down, she saw his crutch entangled in her dupatta. Calmly pulling it from her head, she tossed it to her cousin, who gasped at the impropriety.

The thousand-odd guests held their breath and kept their silence as they waited to see what happened next. Ignoring them, Ananya stayed focussed on Arvin. Sliding an arm around him, she supported his weight until he regained his balance on the crutches.

When he was steady again, she started to walk. Neither of them looked at each other. Neither of them spoke. They completed their pheras like that, together but separate.

Ananya thought her eyes would roll back in her head if the elderly couple continued to list their various age-related ailments. They'd started with bad hearing, moved on to creaky knees and were now, heaven help her, on incontinence.

She kept a polite smile and gulped down some more wine. Somewhere at the back of her mind, she knew she had had enough to drink, but that didn't stop her from reaching for the glass again.

'Hi, sweetheart.' Arvin stood at their table, smiling down at her. 'Enjoying yourself?'

Sweetheart? Ananya was still processing the endearment when Arvin moved forward to drape an arm across her shoulders. Ananya stiffened. He hadn't tried touching her since that awful day, in the bathroom, and she hoped he didn't plan to try anything of that sort now.

She introduced Arvin to the startled couple. He smiled and started making polite conversation with them, exhibiting the charm he was famous for. Ananya let her mind wander even as she chipped in with an occasional murmur of agreement that seemed to be all that was required of her.

'My wife is incredible.'

The unlikely statement jolted her out of her almost trance-like state and had her turning to look at Arvin. He was still smiling at the couple seated in front of them, but she felt a chill run down her spine. She knew that look in his eyes. It had never boded well for her in the past and she doubted today would be any exception.

Ananya slowly straightened in her chair and started paying attention to the conversation swirling around her. She was pretty drunk, but she was going to need her wits about her for whatever came next.

Mr Khanna, seated across from her, beamed. 'What a lovely couple the two of you make. The key to a successful marriage is showing appreciation for your spouse and you obviously know how to do that.'

'Oh, yes.' Arvin smiled, a distinctive shark-like smile. Her fingers clenched into a fist in her lap. Arvin glanced down and noticed. His smile widened and he reached for her fist. Unclenching it, even though she resisted, he weaved his fingers through hers. 'Appreciation is key. I appreciate so many things about my lovely wife. She's the reason for almost everything that's happened in my life.'

'Treasure it, my boy. Nowadays, youngsters have forgotten how to give their partners credit.'

'Credit? I give her credit for everything. A car accident, an amputation, bankruptcy…you name it, she's responsible for it all. Right, Ananya?'

Ananya stared at him uncomprehendingly. What was going on? Less than an hour ago, they'd been maintaining their painfully civil attempt at working on their marriage and now…now the Arvin she'd lived with for so many years had made a sudden comeback.

It slowly dawned on the couple sitting in front of them that this conversation wasn't going quite the way they envisaged.

'Having a bit of a spat, are you?' The old man tried adding a bit of genial bluster to his voice. 'Maybe my wife and I should give the two of you some privacy.'

'Oh, no need.' Arvin's soft voice halted them just when they were about to rise from their chairs. They stopped, bent at the waist, making an almost comical picture. 'No need at all.'

Then, he looked directly at her and said, 'Hello, Anni.'

The bottom dropped out of her world when she looked in his eyes. The fury, hurt and bitterness was palpable. Ananya felt a strange calm descending over her. Finally, it was all out in the open.

Dimly, she heard the old man ask his wife, 'Is Anni her pet name?'

Aware that the family hadn't still recovered from the last scandal attached to its name, Ananya tightened her grip on his hand.

'Not here,' she pleaded softly. 'Don't cause a scene.'

'A scene?' Arvin leaned back in his seat, a picture of casual elegance and sophistication. 'Why in the world would I cause a scene? It's not like I just found out that my wife is in love with another man. That's old news.'

Background noise. There was so much background noise. Glasses clinking, loud laughter, the screaming in her head. So much noise. She shut her eyes in a bid to shut it all out.

'Finding out that the other man is my own brother is fresh news though.'

Arvin squeezed the hand he was holding as he made the announcement. Ananya gasped, pain shooting through her fingers and radiating up her arm. The old couple across from them had frozen in their places.

People at neighbouring tables were slowly starting to turn towards them as whispers spread like wildfire through the gathering. A hush descended on the room as everyone watched to see what would happen next.

'So tell me, sweetheart, how is Anni different from Ananya?'

Ananya didn't answer. She kept her head down and her

gaze trained on the silverware carefully arranged on the table in front of her.

'I believe you already told me. Anni is loved like Ananya is not. Well loved?' He laughed. There was a coarse edge to that sound. 'Did he love you in every position listed in the *Kama Sutra*?'

Tears stung her eyes, but she didn't let them roll down her cheeks. She straightened in her chair. She took a deep breath and looked at Arvin. He sat, slouched in his chair, with an insolent smile on his face.

She held his gaze, refusing to let him intimidate her. Ananya made one last attempt to retain some dignity. 'Can we finish this at home?'

Arvin sprang from his seat to stand. The table wobbled with his sudden, violent movement. He gave her a mocking bow. 'Sure, my love. Let's go.'

Ananya rose, her legs shaking. Conscious of every eye on them, she kept her own gaze on the door and walked with her head held high. Arvin followed without another word until they reached the door.

Ananya had one hand on the handle of the door and was about to open the panel when he asked, 'So tell me, sweetheart, was it worth it? I believe another way of asking is "is the fucking you're getting worth the fucking you're getting?" Or in your case the fucking you're about to get.'

She froze, one hand still clutching the handle. There was pin drop silence at her back. It sounded like their captive audience was holding their collective breath.

The thought rang dimly in her head. There was no going back from this. This was true for all three of them. With a deep breath, she turned and proceeded to fan the flames

Arvin had already ignited.

'Yes.' She thought she heard a loud gasp, but she kept her eyes trained on Arvin, refusing to look away as she imploded their lives once and for all. 'Yes, the fucking I got was worth it. I don't regret it. I don't regret *him*.'

Something moved in Arvin's eyes, something ineffable, but it was gone before she could identify it. He traced one excruciatingly gentle finger down her cheek.

'Did you enjoy it then? Making a fool of me, laughing at the cripple, rescuing the useless son, saving me from myself? What was the plan? Make me so grateful that I wouldn't mind the two of you riding off into the sunset together?'

Ananya moved his hand away from her face, a deliberate gesture that had his eyes darkening.

'Does he know about the guy you were in love with when you married me?' he mocked. 'Does he know how easily he can be replaced?'

'He is the guy I was in love with when I married you.'

There was a loud crash in the background, but neither Ananya nor Arvin turned to look.

'Arnav...' he said softly, 'Arnav was the guy you wanted to call off the wedding for?'

Ananya nodded. It felt like the weight of the world had just rolled off her shoulders. As she stood in the rubble of what was left of her life, she felt free.

Finally, there were no more secrets. Finally, she could breathe again.

'Maaaaa.' Arvin dragged her through the drawing room of the flat they were currently staying in and flung her onto the sofa. Ananya landed in a dishevelled heap, her dress riding up against her thighs.

The car ride home had been horrifyingly reminiscent of the one that had ended in their accident all those years ago. She was still struggling to control her fear and panic from Arvin's reckless driving. This time, she had thought neither of them would survive.

'Why are you shouting?' Shayla came into the room with Akhilesh behind her. 'Are you drunk?'

'Do I look drunk?' Arvin turned to face them, his volume increasing with every word.

'No,' Shayla frowned. 'But you don't look okay either.'

'What is all this ruckus about? Having a fight, are you?' Akhilesh grumbled. 'I'm going to bed. I don't have time to waste on their marital spats.'

'She's having an affair with Arnav. Do you have time to waste on that?'

Akhilesh froze at the threshold of the room. Shayla dropped into the chair opposite to where Ananya slumped like a puppet with its strings cut.

'That's right,' Arvin sneered. 'Your son and your daughter-in-law have been fucking each other under your roof. The only problem is, it's the wrong son.'

'No…no…NO!' Shayla's voice rose with each word. 'Ananya and Arnav would never do that.'

She came over to Ananya and dragged her to her feet. 'Ananya beta, look at me. This is not true. Tell me it's not true.'

'It's true,' Ananya answered, her voice barely more than a whisper. 'It's all true.'

Shayla's hands fell away from her shoulders. 'How could you?' The hurt in her voice stabbed at Ananya like an ice pick.

Akhilesh stayed silent, his face watchful, looking at Arvin. Nobody spoke for several awful minutes. The doorbell rang loudly, breaking the painful silence that had enveloped the room.

Ananya watched with barely concealed horror as Arvin opened the door to let her parents in.

'Arvin, please.' The whispered plea was lost in the cacophony of noise that erupted in the room, everyone talking all at once.

'Will somebody please tell us what is going on?' her father roared. 'It's four in the morning. I thought someone was dying when Arvin called and asked us to come.'

When had he had the time to make the call? Ananya wondered. When had he had the time to plan the final nail in her coffin?

Shayla spoke up, 'Apparently, your daughter is having an affair.'

'What?' Ananya's father frowned. 'What affair? What rubbish! Ananya would never do that.'

'She is,' Akhilesh drawled from his corner. 'With Arnav, our elder son.'

Ananya's heart fluttered like a trapped bird in her chest. Her father turned to face her, his face livid. She didn't dare look at her mother.

'You...' For once, the most prominent lawyer in Delhi seemed to be at a loss for words.

'Papa, I—'

'No,' he shook his head. 'No.' And with that, he turned his back on her and went to stare out the window. It was like the sight of her was too much for him.

'Ma,' she turned to her mother. Where her father had been indifferent, her mother had treated her with a casual, careless affection whenever she'd seen her, which hadn't been often. Her mother believed that children should be seen and heard as little as possible.

'Ma, please let me explain.'

'Explain what?' Her mother looked stunned. 'How can you explain this?'

Ananya didn't answer. She didn't have an answer. No one in this room would understand. Had she been in their place, she, too, wouldn't have understood. Shoulders sagging, she sat down on the sofa again. It felt like her feet would never support her weight again.

'Get up.' Arvin dragged her to her feet again. 'Get up, get your things and get out. Go back with your parents now.'

'No,' her father said, still not looking at her. 'The doors of our home are closed to her.'

Ananya shut her eyes against the pain of that statement.

It didn't stop Arvin from yanking her to her feet. He hauled her down the short corridor to the room they shared. Opening the cupboards there, he started throwing her clothes on the bed.

'Arvin.' Shayla had followed them. 'It's four in the morning. Where will she go?'

'I don't care. I just want her out of here.' He threw a suitcase on the bed and started stuffing her belongings in it. Shayla left the room in a rush, presumably to bring Akhilesh to help.

'Don't,' Ananya said, finally finding her voice. 'I don't want any of that.'

She walked past him, picking up her laptop and her work files. She collected her original documents, along with her passport, PAN and other papers, and stuffed them all into her laptop bag. Without another word, she walked out of their bedroom and back into the hall, where both his and her parents stood frozen like statues.

Nobody spoke as she walked to the front door and hauled it open. Slinging her purse on one shoulder, she turned to face them.

'I'm sorry I hurt you,' she held Arvin's furious gaze and ignored the rest, 'all of you. I'll apologize for the pain I've caused all of you, but I won't apologize for him. I won't apologize for knowing him, for loving him.'

Arvin seemed to have turned to stone. He stared at her unflinchingly, his eyes boring into her.

'I didn't ask for this. For any of this. When we got engaged,' Ananya's breathing hitched, 'I was so excited. I thought we were going to be so happy together. I had all these plans, hopes and dreams…'

She pressed a hand to her churning stomach to try and calm it. 'I met Arnav through you. I don't know when I fell in love with him or how. It was so sudden and yet I feel like I've loved him all my life. I wanted to call off the wedding. I didn't want to be unfair to you and, as unpleasant as it would have been, I still wanted to do right by all three of us.'

Neither Arvin nor Ananya looked away from each other. 'Then the accident happened and I held myself responsible. I know you did, too. I married you because I wanted to right the wrong I'd done. Arnav and I never set eyes on each other from the day you and I got married to the day he walked in to the house a month ago. We were never in contact with each other. I wanted to be the best possible wife I could be. I wanted to be everything you wanted and needed.'

She paused to take a shaky breath. 'But you didn't want or need anything from me. The very sight of me seemed to bring out the worst in you. Your resentment and my guilt made horrible bed partners. Our marriage was cold and unfeeling at best, and abusive at worst. My presence in your life caused you pain and you retaliated by causing me pain, too. I should have left. I realize that now. I should have left a long time ago, but I stayed.'

Her fingers vised around her laptop bag. 'I stayed because I thought that by choosing you, by choosing what was right, I could make everything right. I thought that by enduring, by sustaining, by submitting, I would make up for the heinous crime I'd committed, the crime of falling in love with another man. I was wrong. I have never been more wrong.'

'When Arnav came home…' Ananya felt her resolve waver but she was determined to finish.

'When Arnav came home,' she said again, 'I remembered what it was to be loved and to love. No one has ever loved me, other than him. None of you have. To him, I'm Anni and Anni is someone to be cherished, to be loved, to be cared for. I never was someone who had any of that, before or after him. In all my life, there's only been him. So no,' she steeled herself to say everything she wanted to, everything she needed to, 'I don't regret him. Nothing can ever come of our relationship. We know that. It's over. We know that, too. But I won't regret it. Again, I'm sorry for all the pain I've caused you, for all the wrong I've done, but you and I both know that I've paid my dues.'

Arvin said nothing.

'I'll leave and you'll never see me again. None of you will, including Arnav.' She shouldered her laptop bag. 'I'll see to it that the divorce papers are couriered to you. I want nothing from you. Nothing,' she added, 'but my freedom.'

Before she could make it to the door, Arvin spoke for the first time since she started explaining herself. 'Five years ago, you crippled me. Today, you've ruined me.'

And for that, Ananya knew she would pay for the rest of her life. She took one last look at the people in that room, the family she was born into and the one she'd married into. They stared back at her in collective anger and dislike. There was nothing left to say. She turned and left, the door shutting with a decisive click behind her. No one stopped her.

It was over. Finally, it was all over.

Epilogue

Rain battered the windowpane, drawing Ananya's attention to the single, tiny window in her small office. She walked over and opened the window. A strong gust of wind had the threadbare window blinds rattling. Huge, fat raindrops splattered her face, making her smile. Ananya leaned out as far as she could and let the rain soak her.

'Didi.'

Ananya turned to face Madhu, the office clerk. '*Haan, Madhu.*' She wiped the water still trickling down her face. '*Kya hua?*'

'*Aapse koi milne aaya hai* (Someone is here to meet you),' he gestured towards the reception area to his back.

Ananya sighed. She reached for the gym bag she kept stashed under her workstation and took out a towel. To buy time, she asked Madhu to serve the client some water and ask if they wanted some tea.

Drying her hair vigorously using the towel, she looked down at the simple kurta she wore and groaned. Water had trickled down her front, leaving some very interesting designs on her otherwise plain yellow outfit. Grabbing the shawl she used as a dupatta, she draped it across her shoulders.

She looked wistfully for a moment outside the window, towards the sky, before turning away from it. She loved Bangalore. She loved the weather, the friendly, cosmopolitan crowd, the fabulous eateries and most of all, she loved the fact that she knew no one here. She was invisible and she'd never felt better.

With her credentials, it hadn't been hard to find work. She had started working for an NGO that ran several shelters for women and children. She had joined the team that approached companies and their corporate social responsibility teams for funding.

Desperate to forget the mess her life was, she'd thrown herself into fixing other people's lives, utilizing all the time and freedom suddenly at her disposal. It had taken less than a year for the organization to realize what an asset they had in their newest employee.

Three years later, she was heading the team she'd joined and through her efforts had expanded their shelters, adding four new ones. Her work brought her immense satisfaction. The happiness on the faces of the people she helped was a soothing balm to her still hurting soul.

With a last flip of her hair, Ananya went to the door to meet her mystery client. There was no one sitting there. Frowning, she called out to Madhu asking him where the person who'd come to meet her was.

'*Pata nahin, Didi. Yahin toh the* (I don't know, Ma'am. He was here only),' he scratched his head.

Ananya scanned the area one last time and shrugged. Whoever it was must have changed their mind. She scraped her hair back into a messy ponytail and secured it with the band she kept around her wrist. If there was no client to impress, she could be herself.

Her standard outfit, nowadays, was a pair of jeans, kurta from any roadside stall and a shawl that often doubled up as a dupatta when needed. This was a far cry from the designer wear that crammed her wardrobe earlier. She couldn't have been happier.

Tucking a pencil behind her ear, she hummed to herself as she went back to her cabin. Just when she entered, she saw her phone ringing. An unknown number flashed on the screen. Frowning, she picked it up.

'Hello?'

'Ananya.' The voice was both so familiar and so unexpected at the same time.

'Arvin?' The word was nothing more than a croak.

'I've sent you a gift,' he said. 'The delivery boy should hand it over to you by today.'

'A gift?' she parroted stupidly.

'Yes.' His voice was calm, at peace. It jolted her out of her stunned surprise. She couldn't remember the last time Arvin had sounded like that. 'Your freedom. I've signed the divorce papers. They'll reach you today.'

'Why?' she asked. 'Why now?'

'It's time,' he said simply. 'It's time for us to move on, to forgive ourselves and each other.' Ananya didn't reply. 'You don't agree?' Arvin laughed softly. 'Would you rather continue to spin in this vicious hurtful cycle of anger, guilt and shame that we've perfected for so many years?'

'I had sent you the divorce papers immediately after I left.'

'I wasn't ready to let go back then.'

'And you are now?'

'I am now,' Arvin confirmed. 'I want to move on, Ananya,

and I can't do that until we're rid of this albatross we call our marriage.'

Ananya said nothing. After a second, she heard him murmur, 'Are you there, Ananya?'

'Yes. Arvin?' she hesitated, unsure if she had the right to ask her question.

'Yes?'

'Are you happy?'

He laughed. The sound so unexpected, it brought a smile to Ananya's lips.

'I am. I hope you, too, are.'

Ananya didn't answer him. She was content. Happy was not a part of her destiny and she'd made her peace with that. She wanted desperately to ask after Arnav, but she bit her tongue hard enough to draw blood. To know nothing about him was torture, but to know anything would be worse.

'Arvin,' she had to ask, 'can you forgive me?'

'I already have,' he answered. 'Can you forgive yourself?'

Ananya stayed silent.

'You should go now,' he said finally.

Ananya smiled through the sudden tears stinging her eyes. 'You mean you have to go.'

'No,' he answered. 'You do. You have a visitor. Goodbye, Ananya.'

On that note, he hung up. She stared at her phone, confused.

And then she heard a voice, which stilled her heart and stroked her soul, coming from the door.

'Hello, Anni.'

Acknowledgement

Behind every book and its author is an army that works to bring it into your hands. I'd like to thank Suhail Mathur of The Book Bakers for not only liking the rawest version of *Wrong*, but also championing it and placing it with a publishing house like Rupa. I thank my editors, Rudra and Sakschi, for answering my incessant questions with good humour and patience. To the entire team of Rupa that has worked to publish this book, thank you for believing in it and getting it out into the world.

To the family who firmly believes that every word I type is absolute gold and to the friends who cheer for me and build me up without reservation, you all are the rock I lean on.

And finally, to my readers, I write because you read. Thank you for all the love you've shown my stories over the years.